Give a man a girly girl in a skirt and he's ready to trip over his tongue, she thought.

"Then I meet with your approval?" she asked, doing a little twirl that made the skirt flare out.

"You look better than I dared hope," William said, then winced. "What I mean is, unless they're using really good facial recognition software, we should be able to insert you, no problem."

This was it, she was really doing this. She was going undercover to find a killer. Wow, she was nervous.

She knew if she were being completely honest with herself a good bit of agitation had to do with the man who paced his office with smooth, gliding strides and a fighter's swagger, and the idea that she and William would be together pretty much twenty-four seven for the next bunch of days.

With luck, they wouldn't kill each other.

JESSICA ANDERSEN

PRESCRIPTION: MAKEOVER

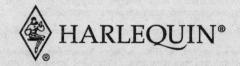

HARLEQUIN®

TORONTO • NEW YORK • LONDON
AMSTERDAM • PARIS • SYDNEY • HAMBURG
STOCKHOLM • ATHENS • TOKYO • MILAN • MADRID
PRAGUE • WARSAW • BUDAPEST • AUCKLAND

To Kathryn Huse, for saving my bacon
with the loan of a laptop.
This one's all for you.

ISBN-13: 978-0-373-88756-9
ISBN-10:   0-373-88756-6

PRESCRIPTION: MAKEOVER

ABOUT THE AUTHOR

Though she's tried out professions ranging from cleaning sea lion cages to cloning glaucoma genes, from patent law to training horses, Jessica is happiest when she's combining all these interests with her first love: writing romances. These days she's delighted to be writing full-time on a farm in rural Connecticut that she shares with a small menagerie and a hero named Brian. She hopes you'll visit her at www.JessicaAndersen.com for info on upcoming books, contests and to say "hi!"

Books by Jessica Andersen

HARLEQUIN INTRIGUE

817—BODY SEARCH
833—COVERT M.D.
850—THE SHERIFF'S DAUGHTER
868—BULLSEYE
893—RICOCHET*
911—AT CLOSE RANGE*
928—RAPID FIRE*
945—RED ALERT
964—UNDER THE MICROSCOPE
982—PRESCRIPTION: MAKEOVER

*Bear Claw Creek Crime Lab

Don't miss any of our special offers. Write to us at the following address for information on our newest releases.

Harlequin Reader Service
U.S.: 3010 Walden Ave., P.O. Box 1325, Buffalo, NY 14269
Canadian: P.O. Box 609, Fort Erie, Ont. L2A 5X3

CAST OF CHARACTERS

William Caine—The FBI agent turned medical investigator would rather work alone than risk the lives of the people around him, as he seeks to bring down a murderous medical conspiracy called The Nine.

Einstein (Ike) Rombout—Highly claustrophobic and rebellious, Ike is a trained computer hacker who has her own reasons for going after The Nine—and good luck to the man who tries to get in her way.

Michael Grosskill—The Nine have someone on the inside of the FBI. Could it be William's former boss?

Maximilian Vasek—The cofounder of Vasek & Caine Investigations has a new wife to protect when things get ugly.

Raine Montgomery—Max's wife and Ike have never seen eye to eye.

Lukas Kupfer—His research on muscular dystrophy is poised for a revolutionary breakthrough. Is he the conspirators' next target, or is he one of them?

Dominic Firenzetti—Kupfer's former partner has a shady past.

Sandy Albrecht—Kupfer's head lab tech loves to gossip. Could she have revealed sensitive information to the wrong person?

Dekker Smith—Sandy's boyfriend checks out... at least on the surface.

Chapter One

"I've never met anyone like you before." Zed Brimley's dark eyes glinted as he toyed with the three glittering studs that marched their way up the curve of Ike Rombout's ear. "You're…different from other women. Independent. Undemanding."

"Clever man. Flattery will get you exactly where you want to be." Ike nestled closer to Zed, who was a third-year resident at Boston General Hospital and her current weekend bed buddy. The movement caused the ascending ski lift to sway beneath them.

She pulled her ski cap down over her ears, which were bared by her pixie-short black hair, and looked across ski slopes that shined white beneath a perfect Vermont winter sky.

Let's hear it for separating personal stuff from professional garbage, she thought as she took a deep breath of crisp air and felt the solid press of Zed's body against hers.

Professionally, she was skirting the edge of some serious trouble. Personally, she was exactly where she wanted to be—taking a long weekend with a handsome, charming guy.

Zed grinned down at her. "Want to hit the lodge after this run? I could use a little something to warm me up." A suggestive tilt of his eyebrows said he wasn't talking about coffee. "First one down gets to choose the position?"

"I vote for the Jacuzzi," Ike said, mentally rolling her eyes. Most guys loved that she'd rather be on top during sex. They didn't question it, didn't make her admit that she couldn't stand the sensation of being trapped. But Zed was one of the ones who automatically wanted what he couldn't have.

It was the only glitch in an otherwise perfect casual relationship.

"Sounds like a plan." When the lift reached the top of the slope, he dropped onto the groomed snow and skied toward a marked trail, calling over his shoulder, "See you at the bottom. Last one down is buying dinner!"

Ike grinned, hopped off the lift and followed with a smooth stroke of her glossy black skis. Now *that* was her kind of challenge. "Then you'd better start warming up your credit card," she shouted, "'cause here I come!"

Zed laughed and called a masculine taunt that was lost in a chilly burst of crosswind. Clad in a formfitting black jacket and thermal pants, he cut a powerful figure as he dodged a middle-aged woman snow-plowing her way toward an easier run and shot down the double-black-diamond trail.

Excitement kindled in Ike's blood—the love of the outdoors, the thrill of speed and danger. She whooped and followed, hurtling along the top element of the run, a stomach-pitching drop that kicked her from zero to flying in the space of a few heartbeats.

She angled her skis straight down the mountain and felt the strain in her leg muscles, a warning that she was getting soft.

But now that things were quieter with both her freelance investigative work and her "real" job as communications director at Boston General, she should be able to get back to the important stuff, like working out. Like acting out.

No way was she letting herself settle too deeply into a rut. Routines were for boring nine-to-fivers. She was all about spontaneity and living on the edge.

Because of it, she let out a yell as she angled between two lines of snow-frosted pine trees and whipped around a corner. *There!* Zed's strong figure sluiced a neat zigzag path up ahead, teasing her. Taunting her.

Ike threw back her head and felt laughter bubble up. "Ready or not, here I come!" She accelerated into the next curve, zeroing in on her lover's broad back as he disappeared around the bend.

She heard a sharp crack and thought for a second that one of the nearby trees had lost a branch. Then she rounded the turn and saw a body sprawled on the trail. Her heart froze in her chest and she screamed, "Zed!"

Going too fast to stop, she tried to turn but hit a patch of ice beneath the loose powder. She cried out and slid sideways, losing control.

Her skis hooked Zed's motionless form with a sickening jolt. Momentum carried her up and over, and the world exploded in a pinwheel of sky and snow and trees. She flipped twice, slammed to the ground and skidded downhill.

She heard another crack. Recognizing gunfire, she grabbed for the weapon she often carried at the small of her back while freelancing. But the .22 wasn't there. She was on vacation, damn it!

The Nine don't care, a small voice said inside her. *They'll get you wherever they find you. Max Vasek warned you, but you didn't believe him.*

Ike's heart pounded, the rapid thud nearly drowning out all other sounds as she tried to scramble to her feet. This wasn't happening, couldn't be happening. *Please God, let this be a nightmare.*

But she knew it wasn't a dream the moment another skier flew around the corner, saw Zed's motionless body and wiped out with a startled yell. A second skier appeared, then a third. She heard their shouts, saw them gesture wildly at Zed, then farther down the slope to where she lay.

One skied toward her, a tall, broad-shouldered man who looked to be in his early forties. He was dressed entirely in gray, and his eyes were shielded behind tinted goggles. He crouched beside her. "Lie still. The ski patrol is on its way."

"Help me get these things off." Ike yanked at her skis, cursing the bindings she habitually overtightened to get maximum speed on the slopes. "I work at a hospital. I can help him."

"You're hurt. You should—"

"Shut up and help me!" she snapped, and when her would-be rescuer tried to press her down flat, she fought him off, dragged herself to her feet and limped upslope.

She elbowed her way through the growing crowd and dropped down beside Zed's limp form. He had a bloodstained hand clamped to the side of his neck, and the snow beneath him was slushy and stained red.

"Oh, God. Zed." She pressed her hand over his in an effort to keep him from bleeding out.

"You probably shouldn't touch him," a female voice said from the crowd. "That must've been a hell of a wipeout. He could've broken his back or something."

Ike whipped her head around and glared at the speaker, a teenaged snowboarder wearing a purple hoodie. "Shut up and call the ski patrol again. Tell them we're going to need a helicopter evac and the cops."

She didn't mention he'd been shot because she didn't have time to deal with questions or panic. Zed was her only focus right now. Besides, it hadn't been a random sniping, one where the gathering crowd would be at risk.

No, there had been a single target, and the shooter was long gone.

"Come on, Zed, stay with me." She kept up the pressure while she searched for a second wound, but it looked as though he'd only caught the one bullet. Unfortunately it was a hell of a hit. She was a computer jockey, not a doctor, but she knew an arterial bleed when she saw one.

"Where's the damn ski patrol?" she shouted, her voice sharpening with panic when his breath rattled in his lungs.

"Almost here," someone said. Zed groaned and shifted, fighting back toward consciousness.

Ike struggled to keep the pressure on when he tried to pull away. "Lie still, Zed. Help's coming."

He cried out in pain, opened his eyes and looked around wildly for a few seconds, then zeroed in on her face. His mouth pulled back in a rictus of disbelief, then worked as he tried to say something.

"Hush." Ike leaned close, trying to shield him from the crowd, trying to will away the grayness she saw creeping over his skin. "Don't try to talk. Concentrate on breathing, okay?"

He reached up and grabbed her wrist with his free hand, hanging on as though he were sinking. Eyes locked on hers, he managed to say, *"Why?"*

Tears streaming down her face, Ike leaned closer and said, "Sh. Just breathe." But deep down inside, guilt stabbed deep at the knowledge that she knew exactly why. The sniper hadn't been shooting at Zed.

The bullet had been meant for her.

Chapter Two

Three months later

"I can't believe I have to wear a coat in my own office," William Caine muttered. "It's spring already. Isn't it supposed to be warm out?"

He sent a glare toward the thermostat, which was set at a chill fifty degrees, and yanked on his leather bomber jacket before returning to his desk, where a computer competed for space with a multiline phone and a pile of papers. Off to one side, a coffee mug overflowed with the pens that seemed to breed in his pockets.

"You got a better idea for cutting costs?" his partner's voice asked from the hall.

"Nope." William looked up and saw Max Vasek, the other half of Vasek & Caine Investigations, standing in the doorway.

Max was as tall and dark and tough-looking as he'd ever been, but these days his craggy features sported new lines, new worries. William had seen the same signs in the mirror just that morning. A recent trim of his short brown hair and a fresh morning shave hadn't done much to disguise the strain.

Vasek & Caine wasn't doing well, and the bills on the New York office suite were the least of their concerns.

Four months ago the company had been a growing enterprise, bringing in new medical-type investigations on a weekly basis. Then Max had gotten himself caught up with his ex and her female sex-enhancement drug, Thriller. The product tampering case had put Vasek & Caine smack in the crosshairs of The Nine, a group of very powerful scientists rumored to control worldwide scientific progress through a combination of bribery and extortion. In effect, they were the biotech mafia.

Unfortunately, almost nobody outside of Max, Raine and William actually believed they existed.

It couldn't be a coincidence that Vasek & Caine's clients had started drying up after that, though. The blackballing was a punishment. A warning, backed up by an anonymous note slid under the waiting room door a couple of months earlier.

You stay out of our business and we'll leave you and yours alone.

Thing was, neither Max nor William took kindly to extortion. Hell, that was why they'd gone into business together in the first place.

They'd met at Boston General Hospital, where ex-FBI agent William had been freelancing for a medical investigations group called Hospitals for Humanity—HFH—and Max worked in a lab. They'd both needed a change of scenery around the same time and they'd both wanted to make a difference. It had seemed natural to combine their specialties into private medical investigations, with a focus on cases like that of drug developer Raine Montgomery, the ex-flame who'd become Max's wife three months earlier.

At the thought of her, William glanced at his watch. "It's Friday night. Aren't you and Raine supposed to be somewhere?" He made the question seem casual, as though he didn't care when his partner left the office.

"I'm on my way right now." But Max stayed put. "Listen, I need to ask a favor, and you're not going to like it."

"That's a heck of a sales technique. No wonder we're down to our last few paying clients."

Max grimaced. "No, that would be the part where we discovered Raine's drug was being sabotaged by a scientific cartel that isn't supposed to exist. Which brings me to the favor."

"You don't have to ask me to investigate the bastards," William said. "I'm already on it."

"I know. And I also know I haven't been much help lately," Max said.

"You've had other things to worry about, like making sure Raine's drug returns to the market without any more glitches." *And making sure she stays safe,* William thought but didn't say.

Though Max and Raine had engineered the arrest of Frederick Forsythe, the man directly responsible for sabotaging Thriller, there were at least eight other members of The Nine to watch out for, along with their underlings. Any one of them might decide to finish the job, which was why William intended to finish them first. His was an ordered world, structured around laws and categories. There were good guys and bad guys, and The Nine were very bad guys.

Problem was, they also apparently had enough power to sway even his old bosses. That was the only logical explanation for why the evidence Max and Raine had amassed months earlier hadn't been enough to convince the feds to open an investigation. Instead they'd decided Forsythe had acted alone, which was just ridiculous. It didn't account for the subsequent attack on Ike Rombout, the tech-savvy, terminally annoying woman who'd helped Max track down Forsythe, and it didn't account for whoever was blackballing Vasek & Caine now.

That left it up to Vasek & Caine—or rather left it up to William—to identify the other eight members of the supposedly nonexistent group and bring them to justice. He'd be ensuring the company's safety and future. He'd be saving the scientific community from their very own version of organized crime. And as an added bonus, he'd be showing up his former boss, FBI Special Agent in Charge Michael Grosskill.

The thought had William checking his watch again. "You're going to be late if you don't get going, and we both know Raine doesn't do late."

William liked Max's wife a great deal, but she fell square into the high-maintenance category in his brain. Not because she liked expensive clothes and makeup— hell, he liked his women to look like women, and that required some mirror time. But Raine also ran a company of her own, and since the wedding, Max had been putting as much effort into Rainey Days as he was into Vasek & Caine.

William understood that a man had to protect what was his, but he had a strong feeling he wasn't going to like Max's solution. Mentally bracing himself, he said, "Come on, give with the favor. It can't be that bad."

"I want to take on someone to help you. Someone who can do the data crunching while you pound the pavement."

William shrugged. "Tempting, but we can't afford a receptionist, never mind a—" He broke off as he made the connection. His mind clicked on the image of a tall, lean woman with a killer body, three earrings in one ear, a mean-ass attitude and a fondness for tight black leather. His blood flared hot, then cold, and he said, "Oh, no, you don't. *Hell* no. You're not saddling me with that know-it-all *Matrix* wannabe."

"Ike is hell on wheels with computers," Max argued. "She knows way more than either of us about data mining and she's got sources we can't even dream of. She could help you find the names. Maybe even identify the next target."

I already have a name, William thought.

I've even got a meeting set up. But he kept that to himself, instead saying, "The Nine already went after Ike once. What's to stop them from trying again if she gets involved?" He might find her annoying, but a woman's skin was a woman's skin, and it was no place for a bullet wound. Worse, a man had died when The Nine had attacked Ike earlier in the year. The Vermont cops had ruled the ski slope shooting a random homicide, and Grosskill and the rest of the FBI had agreed, but Max, William and Ike knew better. They knew it had been a warning from The Nine. *Stay out of our business or else.*

Max grimaced. "Trust me, I don't want her involved. But she's got another opinion."

"Now there's a surprise," William muttered, leaning back in his chair. As far as he could tell, Ike Rombout was all about opinions. "And in case you missed it the first time, no. I don't care how good she is with the tech stuff, I don't want her anywhere near The Nine." *And I don't want her anywhere near me.*

He wasn't sure where the thought came from, but it struck a chord. Ike wasn't his type of woman—she was too brash and in-your-face. And she wasn't his idea of a coworker for a potentially dangerous op—she had breasts.

He wasn't proud of the chauvinism, but he figured he had a damn good reason for it.

"She'll stay in Boston, I promise," Max persisted. "Give her some data to crunch, some leads to dead end, I don't care. Just let her feel involved. She needs this, William. They killed someone she cared about."

That resonated, but William was no fool. "If all you wanted was some long-distance data crunching, you would've just turned her loose. Hell, that was how she found Forsythe for you. So give. What do you want from me?"

Max grimaced. "I need you to keep her busy and I need you to make sure she stays in Boston."

A chill skittered through William. "You don't think she'd actually go looking for—" He broke off and muttered a curse. "Of course she would. Hell. I don't have time for this." He glanced at Max. "And neither do you. But you're still trying to save her from herself, aren't you?"

Max shrugged, rueful amusement tugging at his lips. "Ike calls it my DIDS. Damsel in Distress Syndrome. I can't stop myself from trying to save them."

William could relate to that, but where Max saved people one at a time, William focused on the big picture, which some-times demanded individual sacrifices in the name of the greater good.

Like Sharilee? a small thought prompted from within, bringing the smell of blood and gunfire and the sound of a soft body hitting the floor.

"Fine," he said before the memory could form. "You owe me big-time, but I'll keep an eye on Ike for you, starting tomorrow."

He already had plans for tonight.

HOPING NOBODY HAD seen her sneak across the dark, deserted seventeenth green, Ike shimmied up the side of the brick building, her breath adding white puffs to the clinging fog.

She couldn't believe she was actually doing this on her own, but what other choice did she have? Educated guesswork and an intercepted e-mail ghost had convinced her that several members of The Nine were meeting here at the Coach House, a posh country club restaurant outside Greenwich, Connecticut. She'd thought about asking Max to meet her, but given the way he'd been behaving lately, all Neanderthal and pat-the-little-woman-on-the-head, she'd nixed that idea and driven down from Boston alone.

It was just recon, after all.

But as she hauled herself up to a narrow ledge of stone trim that ran most of the way around the second story of the brick building, her doubts crowded closer. She was a computer geek; she wasn't trained for this sort of thing. Sure, she'd done sur-veillance before, both for freelance gigs and for HFH. And, yeah, she'd been on the edge of the action once or twice, even before Max had stumbled over evidence indicating that The Nine really existed.

This time, though, she was on her own. There was no employer backing her, nobody waiting for her to check in.

You've got your gun, she told herself. *You can handle this.* More importantly, she *had* to handle it. Zed deserved more than he'd gotten in the way of justice. She owed him.

Taking a breath of damp air that threatened rain, she edged across the brick wall. A series of lights set high on the building were tilted to illuminate the golf course beyond, their beams furred with mist. That same mist slicked her hand- and footholds as she pressed herself against the flat surface and began to move, using her black-gloved fingers to grip a thin pipe overhead while she clung to the narrow stone ledge by the toes of her black rubber-soled running shoes.

Her destination was a half-open window about fifty feet away. Based on her assessment of downloaded blueprints, the window should open into the meeting space. Even better, the rear wing angled off the main building near the window, forming a corner where she could fade into the shadows.

Score one for all black, Ike thought, comfortable in her trademark tight dark clothes, one of the few constants she allowed herself.

"Over here," a male voice said unexpectedly from below.

Ike froze. Too late she heard the sound of footsteps on wet pavement.

Pressing herself against the building, heart hammering, she held her breath and tried to become one with the rough bricks.

Don't look up, she thought. *Please don't look up.*

"You got the stuff?" a second male voice asked, higher and a little nasal.

"You got the cash?"

She relaxed slightly at the sound of crinkling paper and plastic. It was just a drug buy, she thought, then quirked her lips at the *just.* Under other circumstances, she might've waded in and tried to scare some sense into the idiots. As it was, she'd wait them out.

She was after a bigger score.

Once their business was concluded, the men moved off. One headed out across the golf course on foot, past the pro shop where Ike had hidden her Jeep. The other disappeared around the corner. Moments later, a car door slammed and an engine started, revved and then faded with distance.

After a minute, Ike started breathing again, though her pulse stayed high at the near miss. She resumed her careful journey, crabbing sideways on the narrow ledge until she reached the shadows near the half-open window. Then she paused and listened.

In the room beyond, low-voiced conversation was punctuated by the clink of glasses. The quiet, civilized sounds suggested the meeting hadn't started yet. Perfect.

Unperturbed by the height, Ike leaned back in the vee formed by the connecting stone walls and braced her feet on the molding. Once she was relatively stable, she spun her black leather fanny pack around to her front and dug out the palm-size telescoping mirror she used at work to look at hard-to-reach computer connections.

Praying she wasn't about to bounce a reflected beam of light into the room, she edged the mirror past the frosted glass windowpane, to the open spot where heated indoor air hit the damp, cool outdoors and created a faint mist.

The mirror fogged momentarily, then cleared, showing her an expensively furnished room, all wood paneling, burgundy leather and a huge Oriental carpet she thought might be Heriz, based on a childhood spent haunting the antique shops of Vermont with her mother and father, before—

She cut off the memory before it could form and focused on the job at hand, angling the mirror and fighting to keep her hand steady as she located three gray-haired men seated at a large table set for six more.

All three were white guys in their late fifties, maybe early sixties, well-groomed and wearing expensive suits in shades of blue or gray. They exuded a homogeneity, a sameness she would have found vaguely creepy under other circumstances. As it was, all Ike felt was a burn of hatred. An ache for revenge. For justice.

The bastards had killed Zed with a bullet meant for her, and she planned to make them pay.

WILLIAM REACHED THE Coach House a few minutes late for the meeting, thanks to Max and his "favor," along with the Friday night traffic between NYC and western Connecticut.

He parked his ride—an ice-blue BMW convertible he'd borrowed from a friend of a friend and disguised with fake tags that matched equally fake DMV records in the name of Emmett Grant. The cover was solid. *It'd better be,* William thought with a grimace. *I paid enough for it.*

The free cover stories were one of the few things he missed about working for the feds, but the money had been well spent. All but the most in-depth background check would show that Emmett Grant was a slightly shady entrepreneur who'd cashed out just before the Internet bubble burst and was now looking to reinvest in the pharmaceutical market. William had the car and ID to match the image and he was dressed for the part in a custom suit—also borrowed— and the good watch his father had given him when he'd left for the Marines. High-quality fake facial hair and a touch of silver at his temples completed the disguise.

He figured he looked like new money and he'd done plenty of research to back up the cover story. He didn't need to have any medical or scientific expertise, he just had to know the money talk, and that was second nature after his years undercover inside the Trehern organization.

When memories of that other assignment threatened to surface, he shoved them down deep and climbed out of the sports car, slamming the door harder than necessary. Then he took a breath and looked up at the Coach House, which was carved stone across the front, ivy-draped brick on the sides.

Unlike his cover story, the building reeked of old money.

William straightened his tie, a splash of lemon-yellow against the suit. Then he said, "I am Emmett Grant."

The identity settled over him like a cloak, an invisible weight that would remain until he consciously dropped the persona. He *became* Emmett Grant, a sharp-minded hustler who'd come from humble roots and didn't mind sidestepping a few laws to get himself the best of everything.

As he walked across the parking area, past four other high-dollar rides, he mentally reviewed his e-mail exchange with his contact, Dr. Paul Berryville.

After Frederick Forsythe's arrest, William had put out feelers through a carefully cloaked e-mail address, pretending to be a businessman who'd heard rumors that The Nine were for real. Over time, he'd filtered out the respondents until he was left with Berryville, who'd led him in a careful dance of innuendo and double meaning that had finally culminated in an invitation. *Meet me at the Coach House at 8:00 p.m. sharp Friday. Some people want to meet you.*

Berryville was waiting for him at the door. The silver-haired scientist's career had been on the brink of complete collapse a few years earlier, when new evidence had conveniently surfaced clearing him of major ethics charges. Now he was the head of a major R & D group, thanks to the power of The Nine.

Berryville frowned, the expression stretching his face-lift-tight skin. "You're late."

"Sorry," William said. "Traffic was a bitch."

"They're waiting for us." Berryville hurried ahead, nerves evident in his quick strides and his silence as he led William through the front rooms of the wood-paneled Coach House, where tables and cocktail rounds sat empty.

"Did you guys buy out the whole restaurant just for this meeting?" William asked, pausing at the base of a flight of carpeted stairs and peering up at the equally deserted-feeling second floor.

"We value our privacy," Berryville

replied. Then he stopped and turned to look down at William from six steps up. "When we get in there, don't say anything. Speak when spoken to and think before you answer a question. You'll only get one chance to make a good impression."

William's scalp tingled with sudden foreboding as he realized he'd miscalculated. Berryville had hinted that he carried weight within the group, and William had taken that information at face value. But a powerful man wouldn't have a faint sheen of sweat on his brow or a nervous tremor in his hands right now, would he?

Berryville was terrified, which could only mean that he was one of the smaller cogs in the organization, bringing the big boys a present and hoping they'd like it.

Hell, William thought as he followed Berryville up the stairs to the second floor, wishing he'd let Max in on the meeting. He could be in some serious trouble here, without a stitch of backup.

IKE PRESSED HER CHEEK against mist-slicked bricks and lifted the mirror higher, trying to figure out who was speaking as words carried to her.

"What do you know about this guy?"

"Not much," a second voice answered, deeper than the first. "Berryville's bringing him in. Says he's a perfect fit."

It took a moment for the words to connect. Then excitement zinged through her when she realized they must be interviewing Forsythe's replacement. More importantly, there were nine chairs, which meant the whole group was going to be there, including their leader, who was called Odin after the ruler of the nine worlds in Norse mythology.

Fingers shaking slightly, she fumbled in the fanny pack for her camera.

If she could get some faces, her computers should be able to match names. Maybe that'd be enough to pull the data threads together, enough to convince the feds that Zed's death hadn't been random, that The Nine were more than just an urban legend in the scientific community.

She eased the digital camera up and over the edge, zoomed in on the men and clicked off half a dozen shots. Then she lowered the camera and used the miniscule toggle buttons to flip through the images on-screen, cursing inwardly when she saw that the tiny, blurred photos weren't going to do her any good. Not even her sophisticated cleanup programs could help these shots, and too much digital enhancement would skew the results so they'd never stand up to FBI-level scrutiny.

She needed to get closer.

Bad idea, her inner voice hissed, but she silenced it with three whispered words. "I owe Zed."

He'd still be alive if she'd been more careful. Instead he'd been buried while his parents and sisters had wept. She couldn't bring him back. But moments before they'd closed his casket for the last time, as she'd pulled the black diamond stud from her ear and placed it in his cool palm, she'd vowed to make sure his killers didn't get away with their crime.

Now, thinking fast, she withdrew a small handheld computer from her pack and pulled up the Coach House blueprints on the tiny screen. She could swear she'd seen—ah, there it was, a small alcove near the meeting room. If she could get into the sheltered nook safely, she should have a better angle for photos. *If* being the operative word.

Breathing lightly through her mouth, she looked down to make sure the coast was clear. Nerves hummed beneath her skin, reminding her that although some of her freelancing had skirted over the edge of legal, most of her work was done via the keyboards and high-speed connections of her three trusty computers, Tom, Dick and Harry.

Until now, that is. But there was a first time for everything, and Ike was all about trying new things.

Seeing nothing below but Dumpster shadows and wet pavement, she worked her way over to where a ladder of sorts was formed by the regularly spaced braces that attached a wide gutter pipe to the building.

She was halfway down the pipe when something metal snagged her fanny pack, then pulled free, snapping back against the pipe with a loud clang.

Damn! If anyone were keeping an eye on things from the outside, they were guaranteed to have heard the noise. Heart drumming in her ears, she scrambled down the makeshift ladder and dropped to the cracked tarmac. Then she froze and listened for the sounds of an alarm.

Nothing.

Relaxing slightly, she shifted her fanny pack, more for reassurance than anything, and headed toward the nearer corner of the building, hoping there was a ground-level door she could slip through. She was halfway there when a heavy blow hit her from behind, driving her forward.

Ike bit off a scream as her attacker slammed her face-first into the building.

"What have we got here?" His voice was rough and a little mocking. "Looks like a spy. Kind of cute, too."

She fought the instinctive fear, telling herself she could handle this, she could. But panic spiked when he pressed closer, his body crowding her, trapping her so she couldn't move, couldn't escape. Fear exploded, making her whimper a protest.

Her captor chuckled and swiped his tongue along her ear, getting off on her terror. He shifted again, pressing into her.

"Knock it off," a second man's voice ordered, sounding older, more cultured, and annoyed. Ike turned her head and saw a trim gray-haired man wearing a dark charcoal suit. He gestured to the building and said, "Bring her along. She may prove useful."

Chapter Three

From the hallway William heard a man's voice say, "Odin is planning to take care of Lukas Kupfer personally before the press conference." Then he and Berryville entered the room and all conversation ceased.

Feigning nonchalance, William glanced around, seeing a wood-paneled room decorated with leather-upholstered furniture and heavy rugs, with an ornate dining table at one end. Dark wooden bookshelves lined the walls, giving the place an oppressive air. Or maybe that came from the three similar-looking men seated at the table, which was set for nine.

William nodded. "Gentlemen." Then he turned to Berryville and raised an eyebrow.

"Are you going to introduce us or should I do it myself?"

Berryville shot him a dark look before turning to the others and saying, "This is the one I told you about. Emmett Grant." He didn't introduce the seated men.

"Has Paul described the proceedings to you?" the guy in the middle asked.

"Not in any great detail," William said, careful to tread the middle ground between knowing too little and too much. "Only that you need a unanimous vote to induct a new member into your organization."

The guy on the left shot Berryville a look. "Then he didn't bother to tell you what would happen if you *don't* get a consensus?"

The threat was clear—William had seen their faces and he knew Berryville by name. Either they voted him in or he'd quietly "disappear."

Even as nerves flared to life beneath his skin and his hand itched for the feel of the weapon he'd left behind on Berryville's orders, he grinned. "Guess I'd better make sure you like me, which means I should skip sports and politics. Any interest in a blonde joke?"

There was a moment of absolute silence. Then the guy in the middle said, "My wife's a blonde." He cracked a smile. "Lay it on me."

And just like that, the tension disappeared from the room. Berryville let out a relieved sigh and motioned William forward. "Have a seat. Get you a drink?" He made a beeline for the bar.

"Sure," William said, glancing at the empty seats. "I'll have a—"

There was a sudden scuffle out in the hallway, and the door opened, slamming against the wall with a bang. A big guy in his midtwenties wearing a black-on-black driver's uniform shoved a struggling, swearing woman into the room.

An older man, neat in a silver-gray suit, followed behind, tugging at his cuffs. He looked up and smiled faintly. "Look what we found snooping around outside."

William was so deep in character that his first reaction was anger at the interruption. Then he got a good look at the woman—who was wearing all black, with pixie-short hair and two earrings in one ear—and his blood ran cold.

Oh, Christ. It was Ike.

She stopped struggling and glared around the room. Her eyes passed over him without a flicker of recognition, and damned if that didn't tick him off almost as much as her pigheaded stupidity at being there in the first place.

William was careful to keep the emotions out of his eyes even as adrenaline flared in his bloodstream. *You just couldn't leave it alone, could you?* he thought with a mental snarl. *You couldn't trust this to Max and me.*

"What are you going to do with her?" asked one of the seated men.

The guy who'd come in with Ike looked pointedly at William before he said, "We can't afford witnesses. I'm thinking we should kill two birds with one stone, so to speak." He held out a hand to his driver, who passed over a mean-looking Glock. The older man racked the weapon, popped the clip out and tucked it in his pocket, then checked the chamber and offered the gun to William butt first.

The challenge was clear. One bullet. Enough to kill the spy, not enough to fight his way out of the room.

When William didn't move, the man said, "Make your choice. Are you with us or against us?"

IKE'S BLOOD FROZE when William looked at her, expression cold and calculating. She recognized Max's irascible partner from the multiple times they'd butted heads at Boston General and from a quick sighting at Zed's funeral that she'd later tried to tell herself was her imagination. But now that she saw him again, she knew her mind hadn't been playing tricks on her. She'd recognized him then and now by the contrast of cool blue eyes and brush-cut brown hair, by the aggressive jut of his jaw beneath sharp cheekbones and by the leashed power in his every movement, which supported the whispered rumors that he knew ancient fighting arts that didn't even have names anymore and that he could kill a man with a touch.

Oh, yes. She recognized William Caine.

Apparently she hadn't made nearly the same impression, though, because he took the Glock without hesitation.

Don't do it! she wanted to scream. *Remember me? I'm Ike. I'm Max's friend!*

Instead she remained mute, paralyzed with fear as he raised the weapon and pointed it at her. He tightened his finger on the trigger—

"Run!" he shouted and fired.

Ike jerked, and for a split second she thought he'd shot her. Then she realized the movement had come from the big guy behind her. His grip slackened and he pitched to the floor.

She didn't stick around to watch him hit. Instead she bolted through the door as all hell broke loose behind her.

William yelled something. Flesh smacked against flesh, and a door slammed. Heavy footfalls chased her. Caught up to her. A strong hand gripped her upper arm, and William's deep voice shouted, "Hurry!"

She would've snapped that she *was* hurrying, but just then they rounded the corner leading to the main stairs and came face-to-face with two old dudes in suits, along with a pair of the black-clad bodyguards.

Instead of slowing, Ike put her head down and barreled between the two old guys. Amidst a storm of shouts and curses, one of them stumbled and went down, deflecting a bodyguard as he lunged for William.

Breath whistling between her teeth, Ike slid down the last few steps to the landing, where the stairs faced the front door. She skidded, hooked a left and bolted for the back of the building. She'd stuck her Jeep beside the golf course's pro shop. If they made it that far, they'd—

"Ike, no! This way!" William shouted.

She faltered and turned back, only to see another uniformed bodyguard burst through the front door and launch himself at William.

The men went down in a tangle, while two more thugs charged down the stairs.

Knowing she couldn't leave William behind, she grabbed for her weapon and came up empty. Her captor had disarmed her. Unable to think of a better way to give William a chance, she reversed direction, charged back up the hallway and yelled as she caromed off the two guys coming down the stairs.

Somehow she stayed on her feet and kept going, straight down an unfamiliar hallway, with heavy footsteps thudding in her wake. Then gunfire barked and a bullet smashed into the wall beside her.

Ike ducked through the next door she came to, praying it had a lock on the inside.

It did, but not much of one. Chest heaving with exertion, pulse drumming in her head, she shot the flimsy bolt before she turned and surveyed her options. Her stomach sank when she saw where she'd ended up. The tiny room was little more than a closet with a bucket and mop in one corner, a drawerlike door set in the wall and a small, night-darkened window.

She muttered a curse as she opened the drop-down door to reveal a dark, narrow laundry chute that presumably led to the basement. *But what if it doesn't?* a little voice asked. *Or what if there's no way out from there?*

Logically, there was a way out, but logic didn't get her very far when it came to small, dark spaces. Her throat closed in on itself, and she swallowed hard as the dark square seemed to expand, reaching for her.

Gunshots sounded in the hallway, along with male shouts and curses. Then footsteps thudded to a halt outside her hiding spot, and before she could brace herself, a shot plowed through the door below the knob and punched through the window. A second shot ripped the lock half off.

She was out of time and options.

Praying the door would hold for a few more seconds, she flipped the rinse bucket over beneath the window, grabbed the mop and slammed the handle against the broken window. The impact sang up her arms and vibrated in her hands, but she drew back and let fly again. The glass gave just as the guys in the hall rammed the door and she heard the sound of splintering wood.

"Come on, come on!" she chanted under her breath as she used the mop handle to punch out the pointy shards of glass. Then there was no time left. The door shuddered, sagged and fell inward, revealing three black-clad men on the other side.

Ike jumped up onto the bucket, grabbed the window sash and heaved herself through. She felt sharp points dig into her gloved hands, felt a pull in her ribs and a slice in her knee—

And was free.

She fell headfirst into a shrub, and the damp branches scratched at her skin, cushioning her and trapping her at the same time. She thrashed as male voices shouted curses through the broken window. Any moment now they'd lean through and start shooting.

Moving too fast for caution, she rolled free of the shrubbery, hit pavement and accidentally cracked her head against the edge of the curb. Stunned, she lay gasping with sudden pain.

Tires squealed in the near distance. An engine revved and a silver-blue car careened around the corner of the building, then flew at her, bearing down too fast. She struggled to rise as desperation flared. She was done. She was dead. She had failed Zed, just as she'd failed her brother Donny, the only person who'd ever truly loved her for herself rather than for who she ought to be.

Then the car squealed to a halt beside her and the door flew open, skimming just above her head. William's voice shouted, "Get in!" Bullets pinged off the tarmac. One hit the hood of the car, wringing a curse out of him. "Hurry, it's a loaner!"

Disoriented, Ike struggled to her knees, got an arm up onto the car seat, grabbed onto soft leather upholstery and tried to pull herself into the vehicle.

William leaned across, snagged a fistful of her shirt and hauled her into the car in one smooth, powerful move as a bullet cracked the windshield. "Your legs in?"

She nodded, head spinning.

"Good. Hang on." He lunged back into the driver's seat and slammed his foot on the gas, sending the two-seater sports car leaping forward with a squeal of tires. He swerved, and the open door slammed into one of the bodyguards, who'd come through the window after her. The man went flying. The door shut. William tromped on the gas again, twisted the wheel and sent them hurtling around the next corner sideways.

Behind them, a limo pursued with lethal grace, closing the gap fast.

William swerved, and the momentum whipped Ike to the side, into his solid form. He nudged her away as he accelerated across the parking lot toward the road. "Put on your belt."

"Right. Sorry." Ike fumbled with the strap, fingers trembling from a mix of adrenaline and fear.

William glanced in the rearview mirror and cursed. "Hang on. This could get rough."

Like it'd been smooth before? Ike thought, her head starting to settle even as her pulse thundered in her ears. She smothered a half-hysterical giggle and jammed the seat belt lock in place. Then, refusing to look down at the ragged tears in the knees of her tight black pants, she braced her feet and nodded. "Let's lose these bastards."

"Here goes nothing."

He sent the car speeding along a deserted secondary road, easing up on the gas. The limo closed the distance and bullets pinged. Then, as they passed a cross road, William hit the gas and yanked the hand brake, all in one fluid movement. Tires screamed as the car nearly leaped off the road, then turned ninety degrees to their original path and slid sideways.

Ike gritted her teeth and hung on tight. She glanced out the window and saw the limo's headlights aiming straight for her. Then William released the hand brake and accelerated. The BMW leaped forward, sailing down the cross street as the limo sped past.

William punched it, heading toward the highway as he weaved through the posh residential streets of Greenwich.

The speedometer edged past sixty, then seventy. Houses blurred on either side in darkness broken by streetlights at regular intervals, and Ike hung onto her seat. At eighty-five miles per hour, the vehicle vibrated and felt lighter, as though it might take flight at any moment.

She heard a low mutter of sound and for a second thought the engine was getting ready to shake apart. Then she looked across at William and saw that the noise was coming from him, a low chant. *Come on, baby, come on.*

He glanced across at her, eyes hard and somehow reassuring. "Almost there."

Then they *were* there. The BMW flashed beneath an overpass, he downshifted and they screamed up an on-ramp onto the interstate. The limo was nowhere in sight.

They'd made it.

Ike blew out a breath. "Wow. That was… wow." She unclamped her fingers from the edge of the leather seat, feeling joints pop. She worked her hands, staring at them. Then she looked over at William's set profile. "Thanks for the ride."

A muscle bunched in his jaw. "Don't say another word until we're back in the office. Then you're Max's problem."

Annoyance flared quickly. "I beg your—"

"You want to walk?"

Ike shut up.

WILLIAM DIDN'T SAY another word to her, not even when they ditched the shot-up BMW, stripped the plates, which looked like clever fakes up close, and rented a Geo Metro under a name that definitely wasn't William Caine.

It was past midnight, and Ike's eyelids were drooping when he finally turned into the parking structure adjoining the New York offices of Vasek & Caine Investigations. He'd called ahead, and Max was waiting for them upstairs, along with his wife, Raine.

As always, the sight of Max's wife sent a stab through Ike. Not because she'd wanted Max for herself. Mr. Macho Protector made a fine friend, but she wouldn't have been caught dead dating him or anyone like him. No, her issue with Raine was even pettier than that—it was how she dressed.

Raine was ethereal. Delicate. Feminine. Her honey-colored hair fell from a careless knot atop her head, with wisps brushing against her purple-shadowed eyes and full lips. Ike had always figured her look was the product of a damn good makeup routine, but given the late hour and the fact that William's call had woken the newly-weds, she was forced to conclude that Raine had been born feminine and beautiful, the exact sort of woman that men gravitated toward every single time.

And that was so not fair.

Ike sniffed. "He didn't need to wake you guys up. This could've waited until morning."

Raine's eyes flashed prettily. "And you could've listened to Max and let the men handle this. Because of you, we've got nothing."

The sting of truth had Ike baring her teeth. "Letting the men handle things is your style, not mine. Besides, we would've been fine if James Bond here—" she indicated William with a jerk of her thumb "—hadn't broken cover. I could've talked my way out of the situation."

She was spoiling for a fight, for something to dispel the residual buzz of adrenaline and the knowledge that William probably would have been an inducted member of The Nine by now if it weren't for her.

He shot her a disgusted look and pointed to a chair. "Sit there and stay quiet until we can figure out how to get you to Boston safely, where your boss can keep you under lock and key in the secure apartments while Max and I worked this out."

Max growled, "And exactly what part of 'Max and I' did you miss when you went in there alone? You should've told me about the meeting. You could've been killed. And now they've seen your face." He glared from William to Ike and back. "It won't take them long to figure out who crashed their little party tonight, and then they'll be coming for you. For all four of us. No doubt about that." He threw an arm around his wife's shoulders and hauled her close, face tight with worry.

Ike suppressed a shudder but said, "I'm far safer attacking than running." And far saner. The high-security apartment building maintained by Boston General, where she'd stayed for the first month after Zed's death, had felt more like a prison than protection.

"Bull." William turned back to Max. "Get her out of here. And keep her the hell away from me."

Ike stepped forward, shouldering between the two men. She focused on Max, silently urging him to understand how important this was to her. "Please don't shut me out. I found their meeting place once and I can do it again. If we combine our efforts, we might manage to pull this off." She paused. "If we work at cross-purposes, nothing says we won't get in each other's way again."

"Is that a threat?" William growled, handsome face creasing towards menace as he took a step nearer her, crowding her space.

Ike shrugged and forced herself not to back up, hoping her sudden nerves didn't show, hoping he couldn't tell that she never felt completely at ease in his presence.

"Merely an observation," she said. "My goal is stopping The Nine. I either work with you or I work alone. Your call."

She expected a split vote. Instead William cursed, shifted, did something with the lining of his jacket and pulled a ridiculously small camera from an inner compartment in his leather jacket. He held it out to her. "Here. I got pictures of the three at the table. You can get me their names. The man with me was Paul Berryville, and as we came in, I heard one of them say something about Odin 'taking care' of someone named Lukas Kupfer before a press conference. E-mail me whatever you find and for God's sake, don't go anywhere alone." He glared at Max. "Take her home with you. I don't want to see her until tomorrow."

Then he stalked out, slamming the door at his back.

BY TEN THE NEXT morning William was in a foul mood. Not just because of the debacle the day before, when he'd lost four months of groundwork and a damn good cover, all thanks to an ungrateful amateur sleuth who couldn't be bothered to thank him. No, he was even more bothered by the knowledge that she was working just down the hall, in the spare office he sometimes used as a crash pad when it was too much work to take the subway home to his spare, minimalist place.

Max had taken her to retrieve her Jeep, which they'd ditched in long-term parking at JFK, and then had driven her back to the office, leaving her for William to watch, which was just perfect as far as he was concerned. Just flipping perfect. There was nothing he liked better than babysitting on a Saturday morning. Worse, her very presence in the office distracted him, getting under his skin and making him twitchy.

After staring at his computer screen for nearly ten minutes with absolutely no idea what he was looking at, he tipped back in his chair and raised his voice to call, "You need anything in there?"

No answer.

A little louder, he said, "Hey, Einstein!" Max had said that was actually the name on her license, and William figured using a name like that out loud was guaranteed to tick off any rational woman.

Moments later, the phone next to his elbow rang. He picked it up. "Vasek & Caine Investigations, William Caine speaking."

"Did you want something?"

He glared from the phone to the door and back before he scowled. "You could've walked down the hall."

"So could you. I don't respond well to yelling."

He bared his teeth, welcoming the sting of annoyance. "As far as I can tell, you don't respond well to much of anything. The first time Zach Cage introduced us at Boston General, you told me we'd get along fine if I kept my FBI nose out of your computer systems. And the second time we met, you barked at me for passing info directly to Cage instead of going through you."

Her voice held an amused note when she said, "I'm flattered you remember me so well. Guess you thought I was cute, huh?"

He remembered the incidents far too well, he realized with a start. He could picture her on each occasion, how her tight black clothes and high-heeled boots had showcased a killer body and how her short black hair emphasized an angular face that was more arresting than classically beautiful. He remembered how she'd glared at him and how she'd stuck in his mind for too long after they'd parted ways each time.

"Don't be flattered," he countered. "I don't like working with people who don't know how to be part of a team."

"Right. Which is why you went to your meeting at the Coach House without backup."

"And I *definitely*," he said through gritted teeth, "don't think you're cute."

He could think of a number of words to describe her, none of which were anywhere close to being as innocuous as *cute*.

"Big surprise," she said drily. "No doubt you like women who wear frilly dresses and lipstick." There was a pause, then a slight edge in her voice when she said, "I don't suppose you sent me…no. Never mind."

William's instincts quivered to life. "What?"

"I said never mind." She paused and her voice went hollow. "Oh, God. Berryville's dead." She said something else, but William was already hanging up the phone and heading for her office at a run.

He found her working three computers at once. On the leftmost screen his snapshots from the Coach House were matched against DMV photos of the three men. On the right she'd pulled up a series of records for Dr. Paul Berryville, including his supposedly classified FDA background check. But it was the center screen that commanded William's attention with a photograph of smoldering wreckage and the headline *Eight top scientists killed in Catskills crash.*

Ike didn't turn to look at him, but her body was tense beneath the black leather biker jacket she wore because they still had the heat turned off. Her voice held dull horror when she said, "A charter jet flying a bunch of scientists to a private retreat lost power and crashed in upstate New York last night. The men we saw yesterday are dead, along with three other prominent scientists and their drivers. Odin wasn't taking any chances that they'd lead us to him."

"Christ." William let out a breath, sickened by the realization that the leader of The Nine had killed his own people to make sure they wouldn't talk. Worse, given that Grosskill had ignored the evidence after Forsythe's arrest, there was little chance the FBI would believe that the mythical leader of an imaginary group of scientific bogeymen was responsible for a charter plane crash.

"He killed his own people," Ike repeated, voice shaking.

"I'd like to believe this means the end of The Nine," William said after a long moment. "But I'm afraid I'm not that optimistic."

Ike nodded. "He'll recruit and rebuild The Nine, maybe even stronger than before." She clicked on one photograph after the other, erasing the men from her screens. When she was done, all she had left was a blank monitor, which seemed to sum up their investigation. They had suspicions but no official backup, bodies but no suspects.

"You got any ideas?" William asked her, their personal differences seeming less important all of a sudden.

"Maybe. Yes, I think so." She hit three computer keys in quick succession, bringing up a new screen on the middle monitor. "I found Lukas Kupfer and the press conference they were talking about. Kupfer is a PhD at the Markham Institute near UMass Amherst. His lab is working on a treatment for a disease called Duchenne muscular dystrophy, and they've got a big announcement planned for this Friday. Something about a new gene therapy protocol for Duchenne."

William stared at Kupfer's file photo, which showed a bespectacled fortysomething man whose face held both laugh lines and sadness. "They said Odin was going to handle it personally. That means we need to get someone inside Kupfer's lab, pronto."

Ike tapped a few keys and brought up the Markham Institute's collaborators list. She indicated a pair of names. "I know these two from Boston General. If I get Zach Cage involved, we could put together a decent cover story, maybe invent a visiting scientist at BoGen who wants to get a look at Kupfer's research. He'd probably buy it."

William grimaced and shook his head. "Unfortunately I don't know enough science to pull off a cover story in an academic lab."

"Maybe not," Ike said. She glanced up at him. "But I do."

Chapter Four

Ike started the mental countdown after making her suggestion. Five...four... three...

"No way in hell!" William snapped. "No way, no how. Not happening."

"What's not happening?" Max stuck his head through the doorway. He was still wearing his leather jacket and wool cap, suggesting he'd arrived just in time to hear William's bellow.

William glared at Ike as he recapped the situation and her solution, finishing with, "Since that's clearly out of the question, we'll have to think of an alternative."

"Like what?" Ike asked, trying not to watch him as he paced the length of the small office, trying not to notice how his muscles bunched and flowed beneath the worn jeans and three-quarter cutoff sweatshirt he'd apparently considered Saturday-at-the-office attire.

Unaccountably she imagined herself tugging at the ragged hem of his sweatshirt and touching the warm skin beneath.

Down, woman, she told herself sternly. *He likes girlie girls, remember?*

Max shook his head. "Sorry, Ike, but I'm going to have to side with William on this one. You're not trained for undercover work, and these men are ruthless."

"More importantly, they know you," William said, continuing to pace. "Odin must've figured out you're back on the case by now, and he'll be gunning for you, big-time. Face it, the safest place for you is back in Boston, locked in the BoGen secure apartment until we get this guy."

"I'm not going to the apartment," Ike said flatly, dull panic flaring at the thought of being trapped in there again.

"He's right," Max said, though his eyes were gentle with apology. "We're not shutting you out of the investigation, but you'll have to run the data from a distance. You're in too much danger here."

Ike saw a flare of triumph in William's eyes and cursed them both for being right. She looked away and pressed her lips together. "Fine."

William tossed her a set of keys. "Take the rental. There's no reason for Odin to associate you with the car. And wear a hat or something on the way out. You're too recognizable."

"Not much of a disguise," she muttered, but she took the keys and started packing up her computers. "I'll call you when I get to the apartment," she said, meaning Max, not the big man who took up too much of the air inside the roomy office.

"You do that," William said. Then his voice went dry. "And we'll be checking the caller ID, so don't try anything funny."

Ike nodded, stifling a quick spurt of rebellion. "I'll behave." But as Max helped her carry her stuff to the rental car, she couldn't stop thinking how easy it would be to reroute a phone call so it would look as if she was in Boston when she was really someplace else.

BY MONDAY MORNING William felt as though he'd already worked a full sixty-hour week. He was pulling out all the stops, trying to figure out how they could gain access to Lukas Kupfer's lab without actually involving a certain someone with lab credentials and research bona fides.

Unfortunately he hadn't been able to come up with a better idea. Granted, the Kupfer link wasn't a slam dunk—they were going on an overheard snippet of conversation and betting that Odin's interest in the lab hadn't changed. As far as William was concerned, that was a hell of a stretch. But as Ike had pointed out the day before by telelink from Boston, the slim lead was a hell of a lot better than nothing, and the deadline to Kupfer's press conference was down to four days. If Odin was planning something, it'd happen soon.

William had been forced to agree with her, though it had grated him. The more time he spent interacting with Ike Rombout, the more infuriating he found her, from the tips of her too-short hair to the soles of her *Matrix*-wannabe boots.

And to top off his irritation, a ten-o'clock appointment had somehow snuck onto his schedule when he wasn't looking.

"Damn it, Max." William glared at the red-highlighted Outlook reminder on his computer screen. "Don't I have enough to do right now without you booking me for a consult?"

Problem was, he didn't have enough to do. Not of the paying client variety, anyway. Odin had seen to that.

At the thought, he checked his e-mail. As promised, Ike had sent him a boatload of information on Dr. Lukas Kupfer and Duchenne muscular dystrophy.

"Now that's more like it," he said, almost willing to admit that she was a solid addition to the team as long as she was several hundred miles away. In person, she was entirely too much. Too tall, too thin, too angular, too in-your-face. Almost as though she was doing it on purpose.

"Okay," he muttered, trying to tamp down a stir of interest. "She's not bad-looking and she's got guts. I can respect that. Doesn't mean I want to be around her."

But if that were the case, why did the office seem so empty, even with Max just down the hall?

He growled under his breath and opened one of the computer files at random, then winced when the technical terms blurred together in his brain. Couldn't she have sent him something that didn't need a translator?

Telling himself it wasn't an excuse, he grabbed the phone and dialed the number she'd called from earlier. There was a funny sounding click after the third ring. Then she picked up. "Ike here."

"Summarize this technobabble for me, will you?"

There was a pause before she said, "And you are…?"

He gritted his teeth. "William Caine."

"I know. I was just messing with you." Her voice shifted from teasing to serious. "You want the short version on Duchenne?

The word *unfortunate* pretty much sums it up. It's a sex-linked genetic disease seen in about two out of every ten thousand live male births. Affected kids suffer from a progressive wasting of muscle starting around the age of three. They're usually wheelchair-bound by ten and dead by twenty." A thread of pain in her voice added humanity to the clinical rundown.

William paused a moment before he said, "And Kupfer?"

"Dr. Lukas Kupfer, age forty-two, divorced from Lucille Kupfer eight years ago. They had one son—Matthew—who died nine years ago of DMD, at the age of ten, which is early for the disease. Kupfer led the initial efforts to cure DMD at the genetic level, faded from the scene for a few years after his son's death and then re-appeared five years ago at the Markham Institute, where he's been working on using adenovirus-based gene therapy to cure DMD."

"Any idea why Odin would go after him versus another DMD researcher?"

"No, damn it," she answered, frustration

sharpening her voice. "As far as I can tell, none of the dead men were connected to Kupfer, his competitors or the drug companies supplying the current DMD therapies. And, to be honest, the DMD drugs probably don't command enough of a market share to interest The Nine."

"So it's either personal for Odin or we're missing something," William mused. He glanced at the clock and realized he had to wrap it up. "Keep digging and e-mail me whatever you find. I have a ten-o'clock appointment."

"Will do. Try not to scare off the paying customers."

Figuring he'd let her have the last word this time, William hung up and sat for a few minutes, turning over the new information in his mind. If she was right about the DMD drugs, then what was Odin's angle? More importantly, how could they get to the bastard if they couldn't find a way into the lab?

They'd already discussed and discarded the idea of warning Kupfer of the possible danger—it was just too damn risky. The man at the Coach House meeting had said Odin was going to take care of Lukas Kupfer personally before the press conference. What if "taking care of" Kupfer meant paying him off? What if the DMD researcher was already on board with The Nine?

No, until they figured out Odin's identity and the identities of the men he planned to recruit to rebuild his organization, they had to assume anyone they met could be a possible suspect.

Out in the hallway, Max's voice said, "This way, please. Can I get you a cup of coffee? Soda?" It was his week to play secretary. Until Vasek & Caine plowed out from underneath the mountain of debt they'd accumulated during start-up, there wasn't enough money for an official receptionist. And, to be honest, there hadn't been sufficient business to warrant one yet.

At least not of the paying variety.

"I'm fine, but thank you for offering," a woman said, her voice soft and a little hesitant.

William stood as Max appeared in the

doorway. "This is Maxine Waterson," he said, keeping his voice low, as though he were afraid of scaring off the prospective client.

And with good reason, William thought as Max ushered her into the office, where she stood glancing from the men to the door and back.

Her rounded shoulders were hunched inward beneath a shapeless green sweatshirt that had cats embroidered across the chest, and her sturdy-looking hips and legs were encased in megamart blue jeans. She wore a shiny brown purse slung bandolier-style across her body with country-girl-goes-into-the-big-city nerves and had her arms crossed protectively just below the embroidered cats. A simple gold wedding band seemed to be her only jewelry, and her long midbrown hair hung straight down like a curtain, covering her ears and shielding her face. As she peered through her too-long bangs with pale, wary eyes, she looked about a half second away from bolting.

The sight kicked William's protective

instincts into high gear. He didn't share Max's predilection for damsels in distress, but though he'd grown up in a rougher section of Chicago, his mother, and later his sensei, had ingrained as many manners as they could.

William gestured to the chair opposite his desk. "Please come on in and tell me how we can help you."

Max departed, but the woman remained hovering in the doorway until William finally sat down behind his desk, figuring his size might be making her uncomfortable.

She edged inside the office, leaving the door open for a quick getaway, and eased into the chair, sitting at the very edge of the cushion. She leaned forward and practically whispered, "My lawyer said I should come see you. He said you could help."

William stifled the wince. Damn it. Peterman.

A few months back, just before Max and Raine had crossed paths with The Nine, William had done a quickie job for Morrie R. Peterman, Esquire, a lawyer with offices down the street. More accurately, he was an ambulance chaser with offices down the street, though William hadn't realized that until later. The quickie job had landed Peterman a big settlement, and now the land shark considered himself one of Vasek & Caine's biggest supporters. He'd hired William for small jobs ranging from medical background checks to photographs of doctors taking "working" lunches in high-dollar hotel rooms. It was steady work, but it wasn't exactly Vasek & Caine's target clientele.

Then again, William thought, eyeing Maxine Waterson, even land sharks like Peterson tripped over the moral high ground now and then.

"I'll do my best to help," he said, consciously gentling his tone. "Can you tell me a bit about your case?"

She was slow to answer, scanning his face with quick, nervous glances as though trying to decide how much to say. Then her shoulders straightened and her head came up.

She smiled widely and said in Ike's voice, "Gotcha."

William bolted up out of his chair, banging his hip against the desk and over-turning the cup full of pens, which pelted to the floor like shrapnel. "Goddamn it, Ike! What kind of a game are you playing?"

She tossed her hair, which was obviously a wig once he knew to look. "I'm playing *your* game, William. And I did okay. Admit it—you had no idea who I was."

He bared his teeth. "That's not the point."

Not even a hint of Maxine's shy slouch or soft countenance came through when Ike stared him down through eyes that had seemed colorless moments earlier but now gleamed an intense, no-nonsense brown. "That's *exactly* the point, and we both know it."

Footsteps rang in the hallway. Ike slouched back to her Maxine persona as Max skidded into the room, glared at William and barked, "What the hell's going on in here? Why are you yelling at your client?"

"Just look at her, will you?" William

pointed, hoping to hell Max would see through the disguise.

He didn't. His eyes slid past Ike's face, which was once again hidden behind strands of brown hair, and skimmed her body, which was disguised in a too-large kitschy sweatshirt and what had to be six layers of long johns under her jeans.

Max looked back at William, eyes hard. "Your point?"

William exhaled sharply. "It's Ike."

She tucked her fake hair behind her ears, revealing a triple piercing on one side with the top hole empty. She grinned. "Hiya, Max. Fooled you, too."

Max looked stunned. Then ticked. But within a few seconds annoyance morphed to speculation. He gave her a thorough once-over. "Huh."

William snapped, "Don't even think it. She's not going in."

Max frowned and said, "Ike, can you give us a minute?"

Reluctance was obvious in the set of her shoulders and jaw, but she headed for the door. She turned back at the threshold.

"Look, just so you both know…I can do this. I *need* to do this. Zed deserved better."

For some reason that ticked William off worse. He snarled, "Just because he died doesn't mean you have to."

He expected her to snap at him. Instead she lifted her chin, shot him a glare he couldn't even begin to interpret and stalked from the room, slamming the door at her back.

IKE WAS SHAKING BY the time she got to the small waiting area that separated the elevator lobby from the hallway leading to Max and William's offices. She wasn't trembling because she was scared of what they might decide—hell, she was going to do this with or without Max's blessing. No, what had her shaking was the rush of adrenaline. The thrill of being someone else. The absolute high of seeing William's face go blank when he figured out who she was.

She could do this. More importantly she *wanted* to do this. It was almost as though everything she'd done in her adult life had led up to this moment. She had the research background to play the role of a visiting scientist. She had contacts at Boston General who would give glowing references for Maxine Waterson. She had the tech savvy to hack into any computer system and pull out the most carefully hidden files. What could go wrong?

The memory of Zed's casket flashed in her mind's eye, showing her exactly what *could* go wrong.

She countered the fear with determination, but even that emotion started to wane as the clock on the deserted secretary's desk clicked past ten minutes, then fifteen.

Tired of waiting, Ike was headed back into William's office when she heard a noise out in the hallway near the elevator lobby. Moments later, the outer office door swung open and an enormous man stepped through. He was seven-feet tall if he was an inch, with wide shoulders encased in a skintight purple T-shirt, wearing narrow designer jeans in a lemony color that was a stark contrast to the gray, drab New York spring day.

Ike's pulse accelerated and she reached

for her midback holster, only to remember she still hadn't replaced the .22.

Before she could decide on plan B, the guy raised his hands. "I'm a friend." He gestured behind him. "See?"

A woman stepped into the office, perfectly dressed, perfectly made up, perfectly feminine. Not necessarily a friend, though. Ike felt a kink of dismay at the sight of Max's wife. "What are you doing here?"

The giant man glanced from Raine to Ike and back. "This is our victim?"

Raine frowned for a second before she said, "I guess so. You're looking…good. Ike?"

Ike bared her teeth, suddenly sweating in the layers she wore beneath her stuffed-tight jeans. "I thought I'd try out a new style."

The giant shook his head. "Sweetie, if that's the new look, I really don't want to see the old one."

"And you are?" Ike snapped.

"Stephen Flores," he said as if she should know exactly who that made him. He didn't bother holding out his hand, probably figuring—correctly—that she wasn't in the mood for social niceties.

Or else he didn't want to touch her, just in case drab was contagious.

Raine smirked. "He's head of makeup and costume for several Broadway productions. Max asked me to call in a favor. He said you need a new look."

Ike's heart picked up a beat. "My look is just fine, thank you."

"Not if you're going in deep," William's voice said from behind her.

She spun and found him and Max standing just inside the waiting area. Her stomach did a backflip when she saw the expression on William's face, a complex mixture of reluctance, annoyance and something else. Something she couldn't quite decipher but that had her blood flaring hot, then cold.

Her voice wasn't quite steady when she said, "You're sending me into Kupfer's lab?"

He nodded shortly. "On two conditions. One, you let Stephen and Raine be in charge of the makeover. New hair. New makeup and jewelry. New wardrobe." His mouth kicked up at the corners. "A whole new you. I don't want there to be any chance of Odin seeing through your cover."

A chill chased its way down her spine, but she nodded. "Done. And the second?"

"I'm going in with you."

She stared at him for a heartbeat before she said, "No, you're not." She looked to Max for support. "You can't possibly expect me to bring him into the lab. How are we going to explain that? And I can't teach him enough science in the time we've got to—"

Max held up a hand. "He's not going into the lab. But he's damn well going to be with you every step of the way. You'll wear a wire and a camera, and if things go bad, he'll be there to pull you out." Max stepped to William's side so the two big men stood shoulder to shoulder, forming a united front that said, *This is nonnegotiable.*

"We'll rent rooms near the Markham Institute and stay together when you're not at work," William said as though it made all the sense in the world. "I'll have a surveillance vehicle outside the lab, and you can sneak me in after hours to look around. It could work. Hell, we'll make it work."

Ike's stomach shimmied at the thought of sharing space with him, at the thought of having him listening to everything she said, observing everything she did.

It would be like living inside a box.

A very, very small one.

She heard a worried sound, realized it had come from her and covered it with a fake cough. She was aware of Raine and Stephen watching her from one side, Max and William from the other.

She imagined Zed watching from above. Beside him sat a teenage boy with drooping eyelids and an angel's smile.

"Okay," she said finally. When the word came out sounding weak and near tears, she swallowed hard and tried again. "Okay. I'm in. When do we start?"

Stephen pointed to the door leading to the elevators. "Right now, because, girl-friend, we have a *lot* of work to do."

A sinking pit opened up in Ike's stomach, but she breathed past it and told herself she could handle this, she could handle the makeover, could handle William. When that breath didn't settle her stomach, she took another. And another.

Then she lifted her chin and marched out the door.

Chapter Five

By noon the next day Ike had decided that the term *makeover* was a myth propagated by reality TV and people who sold cosmetics and home gyms. It wasn't about being made over at all. It was about being unmade, about being stripped of uniqueness and turned into some *Pretty Woman* stereotype.

And even though she knew that was the whole point, there was a line she wasn't willing to cross.

"No way." She leaned back in the salon chair and heard a crinkle of protest from the tinfoil the stylist had folded into her newly extended hair. When Stephen kept coming at her, she cupped a hand over her right ear beneath the foils. "The earrings stay. Nonnegotiable."

"It's not permanent," the big makeup artist said in his unexpectedly soft voice. Today's T-shirt, worn over silver-toned pants, sported a turquoise happy face, but Ike wasn't smiling.

She shook her head. "Look, I've given in on everything else." Maybe not always gracefully, but she'd given in. "I've let you pick new clothes from the skin out, I've put up with hair extensions, a new makeup regime and lectures on how to walk, talk and act."

The worst part was that, unlike the makeover reality shows where the producers kept their victim away from mirrors until it was time to unveil the finished product, Stephen and his minions had let her watch each stage of the unmaking, and she'd seen herself gradually disappear. Everything that made her unique and different, everything that made her stand out from the crowd and made her who she was…it was all gone. No more spiky black hair or tight clothes, no more swagger or attitude.

No more Ike Rombout.

She swallowed past a lump in her throat and continued, "My head is spinning, and I'm going to be paying off my credit card until well into next year. I'm not backing out, not by a long shot, so if that was Caine's plan, it failed. But I've got to draw the line somewhere, and this is it. The earrings stay. Work the hair around them or something."

She'd meant that last sentence to come out like an order, but it ended up sounding like a plea, one that had Stephen's eyes darkening with speculation as he said, "Why? Do they remind you of a man?"

Picturing Donny, who'd had more guts than any two grown men she'd ever met, she touched the stud in the middle of the three piercings. The clear diamond had a small blue inclusion at its center, making the stone more beautiful for its flaw. "Yeah, sort of. The middle one is for my brother. The bottom one was a gift from my parents a long time ago. And the top one…" She trailed off as her fingers found the blank spot where the glittering black diamond used to rest. "It's a work in progress."

The original stud lay in Zed's casket. She'd buy herself another once his killer was brought to justice.

Stephen touched her arm through the stylist's plastic cape. "They'll still be in your heart. And I bet your family wants you to come home safe. Right, *chica?*"

Her parents had no idea who she was or what she was doing, but the pain of that estrangement had long ago faded to a dull ache, and Ike didn't want to go there. Instead she said, "Don't call me *chica*. You're no more Latin than I am."

At least she didn't think he was. Raine's makeup artist friend seemed to morph among characters on a nearly constant basis, sliding seamlessly from fabulous gay man to slightly seedy hipster to Latin lover without pause. She didn't know which one was the real Stephen Flores, but did it really matter? The point was that she believed each of the chameleon roles when it was in front of her. He was, in his own way, a master of disguise, changing her perception with a shift in posture and voice.

And, damn it, he was right about the earrings.

She held out for a moment longer before she exhaled on a sigh that felt as if it came up from her now-painted toes. "Right." She undid the earrings, pulled them free and tucked them in her jeans pocket beneath the cape, leaving her earlobe feeling naked and exposed. "What's next?"

He didn't gloat, merely pointed to the shampoo station. "First we rinse. Then we talk about a name for your character while we cover up those holes in your ear."

But by the time Stephen and the stylist had rinsed the gunk out of her hair, they'd gotten caught up in a deep discussion about bangs and layers and seemed to forget about her name. That was a good thing, because as Ike watched her new hair take shape in the mirror, she felt the panic build.

The long tresses were significantly lighter than her trademark blue-black, and the honey-brown waves glowed with highlights of auburn and gold. Wisps framed her face, making it look soft and feminine beneath the light touch of blush and eye shadow Stephen had assured her would take no time at all to apply each morning.

Ike, whose normal makeup routine was limited to a swipe of waterproof black mascara, had been skeptical. Now, looking at the nearly finished product, she had to swallow a bubble of panic.

She looked familiar, damn it. Not like herself but like her childhood memories of her mother, before Donny's long string of illnesses had taken their toll. She looked like a member of her own family, which was something she hadn't been in many years.

As she blinked hard, Stephen crouched down so their faces were level in the big mirror. "You look great, hon. You'll *do* great. As long as you remember to play your part, nobody'll make the connection between Ike Rombout and this woman." He squeezed her shoulders, partly in support, partly in warning. "Speaking of which," he continued, "what have you decided to name her?"

This isn't permanent, Ike told herself when a big knot threatened to block off her throat and steal her breath. *It's an act. A job. You can do this. You have to do this. For Zed. For everyone else who's been hurt by The Nine.*

"Eleanor," she said finally, and her voice cracked on the word. "My name is Eleanor."

"ELEANOR ROTH?" MAX shuffled through the IDs, credit cards and other assorted paperwork on William's cluttered desk, nearly dumping the cup of pens in the process. "Did you pick that or did she?"

William snorted. "She did, of course. If it'd been up to me, I would've gone with something more appropriate."

He shoved the pens to the other side of the desk and turned the cup so the FBI logo faced away from him. Max liked him to have the cup on the desk to impress the clients, but that didn't mean William should have to look at the damn thing every day and remember that Michael Grosskill was still in charge.

"Like what?"

It took him a moment to remember they'd been talking about Ike's name. He shrugged. "I'm not sure, maybe Spike or Killer. An Eleanor is soft and feminine, which Ike is definitely not."

That earned him a sidelong look from Max. "You don't think Ike is manly, and we both know it."

Wincing at the thought that his partner had picked up on the subtle sexual tension that seemed to be growing between him and Ike, William said, "You're right, she's not masculine. She's a very attractive woman."

"So what's the problem?"

"There's no problem." When Max simply sat on the corner of his desk, waiting, William exhaled. "Okay, you're right, there's a problem. But it's with me, not her. At least not directly."

He pushed away from the desk, stood and moved to stare out the window, not because he particularly cared about the cityscape beyond or the gray sky and falling rain but because he needed to move, needed to do something to burn off a sudden spurt of restlessness. "I haven't told you much about why I left the Bureau."

"I figured you'd talk about it when you

were ready," Max said. "I know you were undercover in the Trehern organization and that Viggo Trehern was scum of the first order. BoGen rumor had it that you were the only one to stay undercover—and alive—long enough to bring him down. You received a presidential commendation and helped put the bastard in jail for life. Sounds like a job well done."

"Except for the collateral damage." William jammed his hands in his pockets and stared at the raindrops splatting onto the window. "It was about a year after I went in undercover. I'd roughed up a few bottom-feeders and put a crooked dealer in the hospital on Viggo's behalf, and he'd started trusting me with bigger things, mostly personal protection. Bodyguard stuff. I'd hit the clubs with him and his boys, sometimes make sure his female flavor of the week didn't stray. Mostly the women came and went, but there was this one girl who stuck for a few months. Sharilee."

He could picture her even now, how her sharp, hard-edged features had fit in with the lifestyle and how her brittle

laugh had cracked at the edges, sometimes turning sad.

"I didn't like her at first," he said, more
to himself than to Max. "What was to like?
She was one of Viggo's women. But I'd
been under too long and I was getting
strung out, starting to question things. There
had already been two opportunities for
Grosskill to move in, but he'd messed them
both up. Thankfully not so Viggo knew. But
I knew." He paused. "I was frustrated with
the Bureau, mad at Grosskill for screwing
things up and, yeah, starting to make friends
in the organization. The lines were blurring
even before Sharilee, but she brought things
to a head."

"You fell for her?"

William shook his head. "No, but we
became friends of a sort. Then one day…"
He pressed his hands flat against the glass
and watched the raindrops trickle beyond
his palms. "A bunch of us were there—me,
Trehern, the doctor he'd cultivated as a
source for pain meds, Sharilee, maybe six
other guys…" He trailed off, remembering
that it'd been raining that day, too. "Trehern

was waiting on a big deal and he was getting antsy. He'd had a run of bad luck and needed a big score, kept thinking this was it, this was the one that would turn the organization around. Guess he'd gotten suspicious, too. There'd been one too many leaks. He knew the feds had someone on the inside."

"He made you?" Max asked.

William shook his head. "Not me. He had it down to Sharilee or the doctor. Played one off against the other for a few minutes, getting madder and madder when they both kept denying it. I tried to calm things down, tried to keep Trehern on an even keel. I was arrogant enough to think I had everything under control, but…" He trailed off, remembering how it'd escalated too quickly. "The bastard shot her dead where she stood. She got this surprised look on her face and sort of said 'oh' before she went down. Just 'oh.'"

Max let the silence rest for a minute, then said, "I'm sorry."

"Be sorry for her, not me." William closed his eyes and pressed his forehead against the cool windowpane. "I was six, maybe seven feet away from her. I could've stopped it. I *should've* stopped it."

"You were on the job."

"So was she. Turns out she was DEA and the doctor was with HFH. It'd been Grosskill's bright idea—a multi-agency op where the left hand didn't know what the right one was doing."

"Then her death is on Grosskill, not you," Max said.

"It's on both of us," William said quietly. "I let it go on too long, thinking I could stop Trehern without breaking cover." He exhaled on a curse. "Not five minutes after the shooting, the DEA came in with guns blazing. Trehern slipped out ahead of the bust, and a couple of us got snagged, but Grosskill decided to keep me under. He let one of Trehern's lawyers get me out, figuring it'd confirm my loyalty if it looked like I'd been put through the wringer and kept my mouth shut." He grimaced. "That was one of the few times the bastard did the right thing, though I didn't thank him for it at the time." He turned away from the window and met his partner's eyes. "I was in nearly another year after that before we finally closed the net."

Even then, Grosskill had managed to screw it up, costing two good agents their lives. By the end of it all, William hadn't given a damn about the presidential commendation. He'd spent a month lying on a beach on the FBI's tab until the nightmares died down and then handed in his resignation. He'd wandered for a bit and ended up back in Boston, where it had all begun. He'd met Max there and he'd found a new purpose, but the work had brought him right back to the same place—watching out for a woman who intrigued him when he damn well knew better.

Sharilee had been Trehern's woman— he hadn't known she was a fellow agent until too late, thanks to Grosskill. And Ike…Ike was her own woman, William knew, and that wasn't a good thing. He couldn't trust that she'd follow his instructions when her own instincts were telling her to do something different. Hell, she'd already come close to getting herself killed. He'd be damned if he sat around while she tried again.

"That's what happened at that meeting the other night," Max said, nodding as he made the connection. "You didn't want Ike to turn into another Sharilee, so you broke cover rather than risking her."

"Yeah," William admitted. "But I didn't get the timing right then, either. Don't tell Ike I said so, but she might've been right when she said I jumped the gun. If I'd played it cool and bluffed it out, I might've gotten her out safe with my cover intact."

Because he hadn't, she was going to be in worse danger than before, going undercover unarmed, untrained and without direct protection, damn it.

Max was quiet for a moment before he said, "Do you want to swap and have me go to the Markham Institute with Ike while you stay here and protect Raine?"

Part of William wanted to leap at the chance, wanted to divorce himself completely from all contact with Ike. But he shook his head. "No, we already discussed that. Raine needs you here—we can't forget that she might still be a target if Odin goes out for revenge. Besides, I'm better with the surveillance stuff." He was better with the hand-to-hand, as well, if it came down to it, but Lord knows he tried to keep that to a minimum these days. It was too easy to let the violence inside him loose, too difficult to rein it in. Still, he sighed before he said, "It makes more sense for me to be the one backing her up."

"You going to be okay with that?" Max asked.

William lifted a shoulder and said, "I'm going to have to be. Vasek & Caine is going to go under if we don't nail this bastard, and Ike's already proven she'll go after him on her own if we don't include her." The very thought clutched an acid burn beneath his heart.

"You got that right." Max nodded, expression darkening. "She's always been a bit of a bulldog, but when Zed died…it changed her. She's harder now, more reckless than ever."

"Great," William muttered, though Max's words only confirmed what he'd already figured out on his own. "That's just what I need. A kamikaze. Well, she'd better know who's in charge. If she thinks—"

A buzz from the outer room interrupted him, announcing visitors. With no clients scheduled, they'd locked the doors and turned on the intercom.

"That'll be Ike and Stephen," Max said, hitting the door release after a quick glance at the clock on William's computer monitor. "He said they'd be here around lunchtime."

A fist of nerves buried itself in William's gut alongside something more, something hotter and more dangerous. He covered his reaction, tucking his hands in his pants pockets and nodding to the door. "Okay, let's go see what they've come up with."

Part of him hoped the disguise was a failure, giving him an excuse to pull the plug on her undercover aspirations. But the rest of him knew they didn't have a workable plan B. At the moment, she was their best hope.

He left the office and headed down the hall toward the lobby, where a man's low-pitched rumble was followed by the soft tinkle of a woman's laughter. Stephen stood in the office lobby, his bulk making the space seem even smaller than usual. Near him, an unfamiliar woman stood with her back to the hallway, giving William a moment to take in the long honey-colored hair falling to the small of her back, the fitted white shirt and softly flowing flower-printed skirt and the shapely ankles and delicate feet strapped into embroidered sandals. For a moment he thought Raine had done something new with her hair.

Then she turned, and his breath froze in his chest.

Ike's heart-shaped face was framed by a gentle waterfall of light-colored hair and perfectly accented with a hint of makeup. Her brown eyes were soft and liquid, and her lips were moist and color-kissed, curved in a half smile.

Lust avalanched through him, vaporizing his blood in his veins and tightening his flesh with a primal male response that simply said, *mine.*

Shocked by his own reaction, William shook his head to clear it. "Ike?"

He expected her eyes to harden and her lips to form the familiar edgy smirk. Instead she tilted her head so her hair fell free of her ears, where tasteful pearl earrings gleamed, one on each lobe. "I'm sorry, you must have me confused with someone else. My name is Eleanor Roth."

She held out her hand, and though there was nothing defiant in her expression or body language, the air between them crackled with an unspoken challenge.

William crossed the room on legs that had gone suspiciously shaky. Before he could process the impulse or stop himself, he lifted her hand and kissed it.

OH MY. IKE LOOKED down at William's bowed head and felt a shimmer of wholly feminine warmth at the touch of his lips and the faint scrape of masculine stubble. *Don't get too caught up in the role,* she told herself quickly, fighting to bank the heat that threatened to gather in her core. *It's not real. None of this is real.*

She pulled her hand away and reminded herself to keep her eyes soft as she glanced from William to Max. They both looked dazed, as though they'd been hit with the same blunt object.

Irritation flared. Just like the secret admirer back at Boston General who'd sent her flowers along with the suggestion that she should make more of an effort with her appearance, William and Max seemed transfixed by the sight of her in a dress.

Give a man a girlie girl in a skirt and he's ready to trip over his tongue, she thought bitterly. *Give him a strong woman who knows how to stand up for herself and he trips over his own feet running away.*

Okay, so maybe that was a tad unfair, but she didn't care. She didn't like the way William was looking at her. Or, rather, she didn't like that he was looking that way now, when he'd never even seemed to notice she was female before.

She wanted to snap at him, but she caught Stephen's eye and saw him give a little warning head shake, reminding her to stay in character.

"Then I meet with your approval?" she asked, doing a little twirl that made the skirt flare out, showing off her calves and the place where a thin layer of flesh-toned latex covered the dragon tattoo that curled around her left ankle.

"You look better than I dared hope," William said, then winced and added, "What I mean is that unless you trip up or Odin has full surveillance on the Kupfer lab and they're using really good facial recognition software, we should be able to insert you no problem."

Refusing to show the hurt that flared at the *better than I hoped* comment, Ike nodded. "Then let's get me wired up. I'm supposed to meet Kupfer in his lab this evening for a quick get-to-know-you chat." Under some pressure from head administrator Zach Cage, her contacts at Boston General had come through with references and a solid cover story, and William had produced all the documentation she could ask for.

Ike's stomach tied itself in knots as she followed the men to William's office, where he'd assembled a pile of miniaturized surveillance devices from God only knew where. This was it, she was really doing this. She was going undercover to find Zed's killer. God, she was nervous.

But as she pressed a hand to her belly and willed her body to behave, she knew if she were being completely honest with herself she'd admit that not all of her nerves were due to her first official job in the field. A good bit of her agitation had to do with the man who paced his office with smooth, gliding strides and a fighter's swagger and the idea that she and William would be together pretty much 24-7 for the next bunch of days.

With luck, they wouldn't kill each other. Or worse.

GET A GRIP, WILLIAM told himself fiercely as he and Max worked to fit Ike with her surveillance devices. *You're a professional*. But that was a laugh, because a pro's hands wouldn't shake as he wired up another pro, and he wouldn't be too aware of each gesture, each touch. A pro wouldn't resent Max as he fastened a microdot transmitter to Ike's lapel and a pro wouldn't let himself linger when the back of his hand brushed against the side of her breast.

Hell, a pro wouldn't even notice that the other agent *had* breasts. But William was acutely aware of the woman standing in front of him, acutely aware of each indrawn breath and the rise and fall of her softly rounded flesh as he worked to conceal a small camera near her collarbone, with transmitter filaments running along the strap of her bra, which was pink and edged with a scallop of soft lace.

He glanced up, expecting to find her glaring down at him, expecting at any moment to hear her snap, *Watch the hands, buddy*. But she stood quietly, staring straight ahead, only a faint blush high on her cheekbones hinting that she'd noticed his accidental caress.

The flush made her look innocent and vulnerable, punching a hard fist beneath his breastbone. If Ike had looked eminently unapproachable and prickly in black leather and boots, now she looked vulnerable and…touchable.

"You almost done?" she inquired. Her voice carried a bit more edge than before, but when he glanced up, there was nothing in her eyes besides polite inquiry.

She was good, he admitted, partly relieved that their half-assed plan might just have a chance of succeeding, but mostly worried, because even if she played the part, he knew from experience just how many things could go wrong in a split second during an op like this one.

Not for the first time, he wished Grosskill weren't such an unapproachable ass.

"You're good to go," he said, stepping back and resisting the urge to smooth down a crease in Ike's blouse. He glanced over at Max and received an affirmative nod. "You're wired for sight and sound, and Kupfer shouldn't suspect a thing." But when she moved away from him, he touched her arm, squeezing to provide emphasis when he said, "*Shouldn't* is the operative word here. There aren't any guarantees, Ike. If things go wrong, I might not be able to get to you in time." He paused. "You can still back out, you know."

She pulled away, eyes dark with an unreadable emotion. "I know there aren't any guarantees. And, no, I'm not backing out. And in the future please call me Eleanor. It helps me stay in character."

"Of course." He dropped her arm and stepped away. "I get that. Going undercover…" He trailed off, realizing there was really nothing left to say. She'd made her choice and they would both have to live with it. "Never mind. Just promise me you'll be careful."

He expected her to snap his head off. Instead she nodded. "I will. And I hate to admit it, but I'm glad you'll be there. I'll feel safer knowing that you're backing me up."

You shouldn't, he wanted to say. *I could*

time it wrong again. I could get you killed.
Instead he gestured toward the door. "Let's roll. We don't want you to be late for your meeting."

Chapter Six

Located just outside the midsize city of Springfield, Massachusetts, the Markham Institute of Biomedical Research was high-tech dressed up to resemble the brick and ivy of the Five Colleges farther north. As Ike pulled into the parking lot, she picked out a pair of security cameras high up in a maple tree by the entrance, providing redundancy for the guard shack, where a uniformed security guard stepped out and motioned for her to buzz down the window of her nondescript SUV.

The guard was in his early forties, with a hanging gut and sideburns that nearly hit his chin. He was carrying a clipboard and wearing a scowl, but when he ducked down to see into the car, his expression brightened. "Good evening, ma'am."

"Good evening," Ike said. "I have an appointment with Dr. Lukas Kupfer."

She kept her smile in place as the guard checked his clipboard, though she seethed inwardly at the knowledge that he probably would have asked for three forms of ID if she'd been dressed in her normal clothes.

The guard passed the clipboard over, along with a pen. "Sign in, please." When she'd handed the items back, he pointed across the parking lot, where two huge brick-faced buildings intersected, forming a small alcove around a pair of glass-and-brass doors. "Go through the door, take the elevator to the fifth floor and hit the buzzer inside the lobby. Doc Kupfer will let you in."

She nodded her thanks and drove across the parking lot, choosing a relatively secluded spot in the back corner. As she drove, she remained acutely aware that she wasn't alone in the SUV.

Directly behind her seat, a polymer screen closed off the back of the vehicle.

On it, a three-dimensional holographic projection made it look as if there was nothing but seats and normal car clutter in the back of the SUV. Behind the screen, though, William sat in a small command center wearing a pair of headphones and a scowl.

She didn't have to see the expression to know it was there; he'd been surly since they'd left New York City, long before they'd switched drivers and he'd moved to the back. They hadn't spoken during the drive because there really wasn't much to talk about. The air, though, had vibrated with the things they hadn't said.

"It's showtime." She turned off the SUV and dropped the keys into her girlie Eleanor purse. "Wish me luck."

She expected a snide rejoinder, but he said only, "Good luck." His voice sounded both from behind her in the vehicle and inside her head, courtesy of a small transmitter that was tucked deep into her ear and hidden beneath her long hair.

His restraint should have soothed her. Instead, as she climbed out of the SUV and shut the door, then crossed the parking lot toward the building the guard had indicated, nerves pulled her chest tight, making it hard to breathe.

She paused at the double doors, suddenly unable to believe she was really going undercover in a dress and heels. She didn't have her gun, didn't have Tom, Dick and Harry or any of her usual equipment. She had a camera clipped to her bra—which was pink, for God's sake—and nothing to work with besides her wits.

"You going to stand there all day?" William's transmitted question was dry as dust, but she knew he was really asking, *Are you going to be okay?* She felt a momentary flare of emotion at his concern, then cursed herself for wishful thinking. In all likelihood he'd really meant, *Move your flower-covered butt.*

"I'm fine," she said and pushed open one of two glass doors that were embossed with researchers' names in gold paint. "I'm going in."

"I've got a visual from the camera," he said with a touch of impatience. "Don't give me a running commentary or you'll look like an idiot."

She found his sarcasm perversely comforting as she entered the building, stifling the urge to say things like *I'm on the elevator* and *I'm buzzing to get let in now.* As she stood in the chrome-and-glass waiting area just outside the elevator on the fifth floor, though, she couldn't help feeling as if William were standing just behind her, smoothing out the jitter of nerves that gathered in her stomach. Figuring what he didn't know wouldn't hurt either of them, she allowed herself to take comfort in the image as a hazy figure appeared on the other side of the frosted glass. There was a buzzing noise and the door popped free of its lock and pushed inward.

The man who held open the door was about her height, shy of six feet by an inch or two, but rang in at about twice her mass. He wasn't fat, more like heavy all over, with large arms and powerful-looking legs beneath a gray suit, white shirt and conservative navy tie. As in his photographs, Lukas Kupfer's face seemed caught somewhere between laughter and sadness as he held out his hand. "Miss Roth, welcome. It's a pleasure to meet you."

She shook. "The pleasure is mine, Dr. Kupfer. Thank you so much for allowing me to visit your lab on such short notice."

"Anything to help out the good folk at Boston General." He grinned, the expression taking at least five years off his looks. "That's the joy of working in academia rather than industry—we get to share the fun stuff."

He ushered her through the door and into a lobby that was done in muted grays and beiges. It held two cluttered reception desks facing away from a wall of filing cabinets, printers and copy machines. Both desks were empty since it was after quitting time, but their surfaces gave the impression of ordered chaos. Two of the walls were hung with colorful prints—fluorescent-labeled cells on one side and schematic pictures of DNA molecules on the other. The remaining wall space was taken up by doorways: four leading to offices; one to what looked like a break room; and an airlock-type doorway in the far wall offering access to the lab area.

Kupfer waved her across the lobby. "Come on into my office. I want to give you a couple of reprints for background info, and then we can head into the lab and have a look around."

His office was lined with floor-to-ceiling bookcases that were uniformly stuffed to the brim with journals, along with enough books to fill a small library, their titles ranging from *The Clinico-genetic Characteristics of the Muscular Dystrophies* and a thin volume entitled *A Boy Like Me—DMD Explained,* to what looked like just about every *Far Side* compendium ever published. The stacked journals, papers and books leaned against one another with apparent disregard for the laws of gravity, looking as though they might avalanche at any moment onto the desk that sat in the center of the small room, facing the single window. The desk surface was nearly dominated by a good-size desktop computer and an industrial-looking printer, along with a Mason jar full of what looked like Super Balls and a beat-up-looking stuffed dog.

Kupfer crossed to one of the bookcases and started flipping through a stack of papers, no doubt looking for the journal articles he'd mentioned. Ike wandered to the other side of the small room, where a few more personal items rested on a relatively neat shelf. She could've told him not to bother with the reprints, that she'd already studied everything he'd ever written, plus a handful of the most recent papers published by each of his competitors. Instead she scanned the shelf, looking for insight into Kupfer, a hint of whether he was Odin's co-conspirator or his next victim.

She focused on a trifold frame that held three photographs, all of the same subjects—a handsome blond woman and a young, brown-haired boy with stick-thin limbs and a devilish glint in his eyes. She touched the frame. "This was your son?"

It seemed safe to use the past tense without giving away her background research. Any Google search would pull up the story of how Kupfer had first started studying Duchenne muscular dystrophy because he'd had an affected son who'd died.

"His name was Matthew." Kupfer crossed the room and stood beside her so they were both looking at the photographs of a laughing mother and child. "He was only ten when the disease took him."

"Too young," Ike said, trying hard not to let the boy in the photo blur to the memory of another challenged child, one with downward-turned eyes and her father's chin.

"I think he'd be proud of what I've accomplished here," Kupfer said simply. Then he handed her a thick stack of reprinted journal articles and waved her to the door. "It's getting late and you'll want to settle in at your hotel. I'll give you a quick tour of the lab so you can orient yourself and then tomorrow morning I'll introduce you to my head tech, Sandy Boylen. She'll help you run your tests."

It took Ike a half second to remember the blood samples Zach Cage had FedExed her from Boston General. That was ostensibly the reason she was there—to use Kupfer's highly optimized fluorescent hybridization techniques to identify the genetic defects in three BoGen patients who had all the symptoms of the Duchenne but had so far screened negative for the known DMD mutations.

She nodded. "That'd be great."

Beyond the heavy-duty negatively pressurized door, Kupfer's lab consisted of five interconnecting rooms along one side of the building, plus a hallway leading to several smaller individual rooms that could be sealed and pressurized as needed, to protect the purity of the samples and experiments. As Ike followed the scientist from room to room, she inhaled the mingled scents of solvents, tissue culture media and floor wax that seemed to pervade just about every academic biotech lab she'd ever entered.

Kupfer led her through a long room. "We process the patients' blood samples in here, isolating the white blood cells and either immortalizing them in long-term culture or extracting DNA for amplification and sequencing. All of the procedures are performed under the hoods, to reduce the chance of cross-contamination." He gestured to a series of glass-enclosed boxes along one wall, where panels could be pulled down to just above a tech's gloved arms, allowing a gentle vacuum to suck up any fumes or debris. Lab benches were set along the other wall, some holding basic microbiological equipment, others piled with the bits and pieces of a working lab.

"See if you can get him talking about the press conference," William's voice said suddenly in her ear, startling her.

Ike hid the flinch and inwardly berated herself for needing the reminder. *Focus,* she told herself, feeling the press of the small transmitter in her ear and the scrape of the wire beneath her bra. *You're supposed to be investigating.*

"Tell me a bit about what you're doing in here," she requested, knowing that most scientists would talk endlessly about their work given the slightest provocation.

Sure enough, that was all the encouragement he needed to give her a mini lecture on DMD. As he talked, he led her into the next room, which was full of cell culture equipment, along with several large incubators. The air was warmer and smelled faintly yeasty with an overtone of sweetness from the liquid media used to feed the growing cells. Kupfer's voice gained volume and enthusiasm as he talked about how the cells of DMD patients couldn't make a protein called dystrophin on their own. "So I've spent the past decade developing a genetic vector based on the flu bug," he said. "Except instead of making people sick, the virus enters the patient's body and tricks his cells into producing the dystrophin protein from DNA sequences contained within the virus."

"Fascinating," Ike said and meant it.

He glanced at her. "You've heard about the press conference on Friday?"

She lifted one shoulder and flashed him a smile. "Rumor has it you're about to put a couple of your competitors at a serious disadvantage."

That was a shot in the dark, but when one lab broke a big development, it was usually bad news for competing labs that might have been a few months, sometimes even only weeks or days away from publishing the same discovery.

Kupfer shook his head. "Oh, no. I'm giving them an advantage. That's why I'm going with a press conference rather than waiting for journal publication. I want everyone to be able to repeat my work and use it in their own studies as soon as possible."

That got Ike's attention. "You're not licensing it?"

He shook his head. "Nope. Free access."

"Dare I ask what you've found?" she asked, suddenly certain this was bigger than just DMD, which would explain why The Nine were interested.

"I've finally found the missing piece that's prevented DMD gene therapy from working as well as we'd like."

"A new viral vector?" Ike guessed, based on his last few papers.

"No. An adjunct." Kupfer's face lit with excitement and he waved his hands as he spoke. "We got the virus optimized a few years ago, but the efficiency just wasn't good enough. Some cells in each culture would produce the protein, but others wouldn't, which meant we couldn't predict or control its effect on patients. So we started looking for a helper molecule that would improve the efficiency of the viral infection and protein production."

"And you found it?"

"Yes." He beamed. "Even better, it's not specific to just the dystrophin gene. Our preliminary results suggest that it should enhance the transcription and function of just about any foreign gene loaded into an adenoviral vector."

And there it was, Ike realized, sucking in a breath. The reason Odin was after Kupfer's work. Not because of the muscular dystrophy cure but because researchers had been searching for a functional gene therapy adjunct for…well, for as long as the term *gene therapy* had been around.

"Wow," she said after a moment. "Congratulations, that's huge." And he was giving it away for the greater good rather than licensing it and reaping the rewards, which could have amounted to millions of dollars, maybe more.

That is, unless Odin got his hands on it

first and managed to license the work, which was exactly the sort of thing The Nine were reputedly involved in. If they couldn't control a major discovery, then they did their best to discredit it, ensuring that scientific progress moved in the direction they wanted, benefiting the group members and their friends, often to the detriment of world health. Granted, The Nine were down to just one, but he was the most dangerous of them all.

Thinking of Odin's possible plans, Ike said, "Aren't you afraid of a leak between now and then? If someone gets their hands on the adjunct and claims priority with the U.S. Patent Office, they could license it themselves."

"Not possible," Kupfer said with a touch of pride. "I may be a touch disorganized, but I'm no dummy." He tapped his temple with his forefinger. "Until the press conference, when the last results are in and I'm ready to go public, I'm keeping the recipe for the adjunct safe in my head. Nobody else knows it but me, not even Sandy, my most trusted tech. So we'll just have to hope nothing happens to me between now and Friday." He grinned at the joke and turned away, saying over his shoulder, "Come on, I'll show you the sequencers, and that'll put us back at the elevator lobby. I'll give you a key and a pass code, and after you've gone over the test procedures with Sandy tomorrow morning, you can feel free to come and go as you like. We're pretty casual around here."

"Far too casual for someone sitting on a billion-dollar discovery," William's voice said in her ear, and Ike almost nodded in agreement.

She covered the movement by turning and pretending to be fascinated with a nearby cryo chamber that had the name *Firenzetti* scrawled across it in black pen, then frowned when the name struck a chord.

Kupfer followed her gaze. "My former coinvestigator, Dominic Firenzetti. You may have heard the story of us parting ways. It was...less than amicable."

"I'm sorry," Ike said automatically, vaguely remembering something about ethics charges, which got her thinking it was odd that the connection hadn't come up in her searches on Kupfer. In fact, Firenzetti's name damn well should have popped, she thought, which meant either she was slipping or someone very savvy had buried the info on purpose.

She didn't think she was slipping.

THE NEXT MORNING, IKE used the pass code Kupfer had given her to buzz herself into the lab lobby just before eight o'clock and was surprised to find the place already bustling. Then again, she supposed they were hustling to finish the last few experiments Kupfer had mentioned.

"You must be Eleanor." A petite blond woman in an overlarge white lab coat detached herself from a group over near one of the copy machines and crossed the room, hand extended in greeting. "I'm Sandy. Luke asked me to keep an eye out for you." She glanced down. "Killer boots, by the way."

Ike glanced down at the footwear in question, a pair of beige stretch-leather pull-ons visible beneath yet another Eleanor dress. "Thanks," she said, thinking, *You can have them.*

When she, William and Max had discussed the plan—or, rather, when she and Max had discussed it and William had glowered his disapproval—she'd figured she could handle just about anything for four days. And she could, really, she told herself as she half listened to Sandy introducing the rest of the six-member lab staff. It was just that she hadn't counted on how vulnerable and out of place she'd feel wearing a dress and fussy shoes, how much it would bug her that people accepted her more quickly and spoke with her more easily than strangers did when she was dressed in her normal clothes.

Unaccountably it made her feel as though Eleanor wasn't the imposter in this situation. Worse, she was starting to resent the woman—she didn't even exist, yet she'd had William's full attention the night before, when they'd checked into a nearby hotel and gotten adjoining rooms with a connecting door. Ike had barely unpacked

Tom, Dick and Harry and started her searches on Dominic Firenzetti when he'd knocked on her door and offered her a fragrant bag of takeout. Knowing it was the dress and the false intimacy of the situation that had prompted him to ask if she wanted to share the meal, she'd done them both a favor by taking one of the bags and locking the door between their rooms.

Over the next few hours she hadn't gotten much on Dominic Firenzetti, but it wasn't for lack of trying. She'd pounded the information superhighway in search of Kupfer's ex-partner and had gleaned only a few passing references. The frustration had kept her awake long into the night, long enough that she'd heard the sound of rushing water when William showered and had noticed the moment when his TV went off and the crack of light beneath the connecting door went dim.

Worse, she'd nearly knocked on the door just to see what would happen.

"Come on into the lab," Sandy invited, jarring Ike out of her unborn fantasies. "We'll get you hooked up with a white coat and get your samples started." The head lab tech led the way into one of the offshoot rooms beyond the main lab, which turned out to be a storage area of sorts, containing enough protective equipment to do a level-three biocontainment lab proud, along with a rack of lab coats in various sizes.

After finding Ike a coat that more or less fit, Sandy led her into the main lab, where they ran the Boston General samples through the extraction and test protocols Kupfer had developed for identifying some of the rarer DMD mutations.

The tech chatted openly as she worked, though her friendly conversation added little to what Ike already knew or had surmised. It seemed as though Kupfer was a dedicated scientist who spent most of his evenings and weekends in the lab and didn't date as far as the staff could tell. Sandy, on the other hand, had a new boyfriend she was dying to talk about. By the time half of the blood samples had been spun down to lymphocyte pellets and extracted to DNA, Ike knew everything there was to know about Dekker Charles, including the fact that he wore size-twelve shoes. Sandy nudged her and winked at that. "And you know what that says about the size of other portions of his anatomy, girlfriend!"

Ike nodded and made the right appreciative noises, but her head was starting to spin. *Is this how women talk when they're together?* she wondered, trying to decide if having very few friends—most of them male—was a good or bad thing.

"Dekker Charles checks out," William said, his voice transmitting through the hidden earpiece. "That doesn't mean he's in the clear, since Odin has plenty of money for bribes, but he is who he says he is." After a moment he said, "At least according to my background check. You can take it a few layers deeper tonight."

Ike's cheeks heated as his words accidentally synced with the conversation and her earlier thoughts.

"How about you?" Sandy asked, clearly settling in for gossip as she competently inserted the DNA samples into a heated vacuum spinner to dry. "I don't see any rings. You got a guy?"

"No," Ike answered, acutely aware that William was listening in on the conversation. "Not right now. I was with someone a few months ago, but it didn't work out." She sent a mental apology to Zed's memory.

"So you're in the market." While she waited on the drying samples, Sandy stepped back and gave Ike a long up-and-down inspection. "Are you in town through the weekend? A friend of a friend's having a party."

"Thanks, but I probably won't be here past Friday." Ike's initial response was based on the case, on the knowledge that everything was leading up to the press conference, but something compelled her to add, "And I'm not really in the market. It's…complicated."

She'd meant because of Zed and her focus on bringing Odin to justice, but the statement rang true on another level, as well. Ever since the moment she'd put on her first Eleanor dress, she'd been reacting strangely around William, feeling flustered and giddy if he so much as looked at her. He wasn't her type and he'd made no secret of the fact that she wasn't his, but the attraction remained.

So, yeah, it was complicated. And getting more so by the minute.

"Okay," Sandy said as she popped open the dried DNA samples and added a few drops of buffer to each, working under a fume hood and switching out the disposable tips to her measuring device to avoid contamination. "We'll give these a few minutes to resuspend and then move on to the amplification step." She glanced at her watch. "That gives me time to run downstairs and grab a coffee in the cafeteria. You want anything?"

"I think I'll flip through a couple of the reprints Dr. Kupfer gave me," Ike said, feeling a twinge of guilt at the deception. "Can I meet you back here in a little while?"

Sandy grinned. "Sounds like a plan."

But once she was gone, Ike didn't head for the desk she'd been given to use. Instead she wandered around the lab, appearing to be checking out the various pieces of equipment. In reality, she was planting the small audio bugs that William had given her, which would offer them an opportunity to monitor things in the lab after hours.

Out in the far hallway nearest the ladies' room, she opened a few doors, still trying to familiarize herself with the layout of the fifth floor. She discovered that one of those doors led to a back stairwell and she stuck her head out and took a brief look around, noticing two men keying through a locked door onto the fourth floor.

She was just about to head back to the lab when William said, "Wait a minute. I need to back up the video feed and check something." There was a pause before he said, "Son of a bitch." His voice was colder than she'd ever heard it.

"What's wrong?"

There was another pause, longer this time, and then he said, "See if you can get onto the fourth floor. One of the men you just saw was my old boss, Michael Gross-kill."

"Seriously?" Ike said, shocked. Then she corrected herself. "Of course you're serious. You're not much in the sense-of-humor department. Which brings up the question of what the hell Grosskill's doing here and whose side he's on."

"That's what we need to figure out."

"I'm on my way." She took a deep breath and opened the door to the stairwell.

"Careful," William said, his voice tight. "He can't know you made him."

She nodded even though he couldn't see the motion. "I know."

It took her nearly a minute to bypass the keypad, and she was only that quick because Boston General used a similar setup and she knew a few tricks. Once the door was open, she slipped onto the fourth floor. The stairwell door opened near a corner where two short hallways connected, with doors on either side at regular intervals.

"Nice job on the lock," William said, an offhand compliment that shouldn't have warmed her as thoroughly as it did. Then he said, "According to the Markham Institute's home page, Drs. Minor Johnson and Karma Leon share the fourth floor. Both of them are on the financial board. Think they might have an opinion about Kupfer giving away millions of dollars?"

We'll find out, Ike thought. She padded across the hallway, where she pressed her ear to the first of the doors. Hearing nothing from within and finding it locked, she moved to the next doorway and repeated the process.

The floor felt oddly deserted for mid-week, making her wonder what she'd find if she investigated the Johnson and Leon labs.

She was up to the fifth door, the one nearest the corner, when a man's voice suddenly spoke from the intersecting corridor. "That's ridiculous."

Ike froze as there was a pause and then the same voice said, "He can't possibly think he'll get away with something like that."

The one-sided conversation suggested a cell call, and only a single set of footsteps sounded on the tile. Adrenaline shot through her bloodstream in an instant fight-or-flight response. She could probably take a single unsuspecting scientist, but what about a trained federal agent?

Hide! She wasn't sure if that was her thought or William's snapped command, but she twisted the nearest doorknob. Locked. Heart pounding in her ears, she tried the next two doors as the footsteps drew closer, so near it was too late to make it across to the stairwell.

The next knob turned easily. She yanked open the door and found herself staring into a shallow closet containing a half dozen liquid nitrogen tanks, stacked from floor to ceiling, leaving only a narrow opening for her to wedge herself into.

She froze, staring into the cramped, dark space.

"Get in." This time she was sure the command came from William, because her subconscious would never suggest such a thing. But what other choice did she have?

Tension vibrating through her body, she backed into the closet. Nausea pressed up into her throat. The walls closed in on her, stealing the oxygen from the air around her.

"Close the door!" William barked.

Panic crowded close, bringing a bloom of sweat to her forehead and armpits, a faint tremor to her legs as she reached out and grabbed the knob of the closet door and… Pulled. It. Shut.

Chapter Seven

The darkness was instant and absolute. Ike heard a squeak and thought for a moment there were mice in there with her, then realized she'd made the noise. She pressed her lips together, forcing the whimpers deep inside as the panic gathered steam.

"If I can hear you breathing, he will, too," William said urgently. "You've got to slow it down—*now*."

She took a breath and held it as the footsteps paused just outside her closet door. Her pulse banged in her ears, so loud she could barely make out the man's voice saying, "…people in place, damn it!"

William cursed. "If I knew you were this twitchy under pressure, I never would have—" He broke off. "You held it together back at the Coach House, when that bastard had a gun to your head. Which means it's something else." There was a pause, and his voice changed as he added it up. "Swallow once if you're claustrophobic."

She swallowed frantically, still holding her breath, acutely aware of the close walls and the darkness. Her lungs tightened, crying for oxygen, but she knew if she stopped holding her breath, she'd scream.

"Okay, Ike," William said. "I want you to exhale, nice and easy. Keep it slow and quiet, and we'll get through this together. You with me?"

She nodded, which was silly, because he couldn't see the motion. He was outside in the parking lot. Except he was there with her, too, inside her head. He was a little guardian angel on her shoulder, helping her relax. She held his image in her mind's eye as she followed his instructions, exhaling quietly, then inhaling as her head spun.

But it was still so dark, so cramped. The liquid nitrogen containers pressed against her body, and dust tickled her nose and throat, making her want to sneeze.

"Stay with me," William said. "Think about something else, anything other than being in a closet."

Which just served to remind her she was in a closet and got her blood pumping again. Panic vised her. She couldn't get any air. The darkness spun and light blotches patched her vision. A rushing noise gathered in her head, warning her that she was trapped, she was dying, nobody would ever find her in this—

"Ike!" William snapped. "Goddamn it, slow your breathing and think of something else!" Then he muttered something and his voice changed as he said, "Okay, here goes. I'm going to tell you a story and I want you to listen closely to my voice." He paused and then said, "When I was a kid, I wanted to be Bruce Lee."

Who cares? Ike wanted to snap, but she couldn't because the guy was still out there, standing near the stairwell, talking on his phone, keeping her trapped inside the hot, airless closet. Her head spun and her legs started to shake, and she would've jammed her fist against her mouth to keep the screams in, but there was no room to move even that little bit. Tears gathered and fell, and sobs welled up, threatening to break free.

"I talked my mother into getting me lessons at a dojo near where I grew up," William continued as if she cared. "I got into it. I wasn't the most talented kid, but I worked hard enough that after a few years the sensei started showing me some extra stuff now and then and giving me some work to do so I could earn extra lessons." He paused. "I didn't compete because it wasn't really about competing. It wasn't even really about fighting, it was about finding ways not to fight."

He paused, and Ike found her breathing starting to slow, found herself focusing on the story as he continued. "Anyway, I was seventeen, nearly eighteen—I'd just graduated high school and was headed for a local college when a couple of punks broke into the dojo and murdered the sensei over a few hundred dollars." He exhaled, his voice going hard when he said, "A couple of weeks later I joined the Marines and learned how to fight for real. God, I hated it. Still do. Problem is, I'm good at it. Too good." He paused for a long moment before he said, "Sorry. I was thinking I needed to get your mind off things, and that just came out. Not much of a story, was it?"

When he fell silent, Ike realized that whether or not the tale had a happy ending, or any ending, really, it had done the trick. Her heart rate was level, she was breathing without a wheeze and the hallway outside her hiding spot was quiet.

Barely daring to hope, she pressed her face against the door near the hinge crack and listened. Nothing. She was alone.

Relief blossomed in her chest and gratitude warmed her. *Thank you,* she thought, not daring to say the words aloud yet feeling a new warmth toward William.

She forced herself to move slowly, turning the knob a degree at a time, then easing the door ajar and listening again. Still nothing. Opening the closet door farther, she slipped out, shut the door behind her and crossed the hallway to the stairwell door, which yielded easily.

She made it back up to the fifth floor on trembling legs and keyed her way through the lock with fingers that shook so much she had to enter the code twice.

Once she was back in the hallway where she'd started, she ducked into the empty ladies' room, where her legs gave way and she sank ungracefully to the floor. "Oh, God. Omigod. I can't believe that just happened. I can't believe I freaked out like that." Except she could. She'd never been good about small spaces.

She pressed her face against her knees, so the words came out muffled when she said, "Thank you, William. You were great back there. I wouldn't have made it without you talking me through."

It was perhaps the first heartfelt thing she'd ever said to him, the first honest, open thing she'd offered him that hadn't been preceded or followed by a dig. She expected him to come back with a sharp rejoinder that gained him points in their ongoing unstated battle.

Instead he said quite simply, "You're welcome."

"I'm sorry I didn't get anything on Grosskill." She lifted her head and plucked at her skirt. "Guess my first full day isn't going so well."

"Your insertion was successful," he reminded her. "Give it time. Hell, I was under for nearly three years on one job."

"I can't even begin to imagine what that must've been like. I'm nearly coming unglued after just one day in disguise."

"Don't think of it as a disguise, think of it as an identity," he advised. "Say it out loud—I'm Eleanor Roth."

She smiled for what seemed like the first time that day. "Pleased to meet you, Eleanor." When he didn't respond, she took a breath. "I'm Eleanor Roth."

A strange sense of calm descended upon her, and something clicked into place deep inside. She didn't become Eleanor so much as she split herself, pushing Ike beneath the shell of a softer, more feminine version who answered to Eleanor.

"Did that help?" he asked.

"It did, thanks." She paused, and when he didn't respond, she said, "I should go.

Sandy'll be waiting for me." She stood and brushed off her skirt and lab coat.

As she headed back into the Kupfer lab, she told herself nothing had really changed between her and William, but she knew that was a lie. She'd leaned on him and it hadn't hurt. He'd helped her out and hadn't asked for a thing in return.

It wasn't much, but it was more than she usually got from a man.

WHEN IKE WALKED INTO the lab's reception area near quitting time that afternoon, looking for Sandy so they could go over the results of the BoGen samples, she found the entire female contingent of the lab gathered around one of the cluttered desks.

Sandy was at the front of the group and she grinned when she caught sight of Ike. "I thought you said things with your ex were complicated." She stepped aside and gestured to an elegant, expensive-looking floral arrangement sitting on the desk.

"What the hell is that?" William asked through the earpiece.

Ike didn't answer. She simply stared at the mixed gladiolas and long-stemmed roses rising from a tall glass vase as ice crystallized in her veins, mingling horror and disbelief.

How had he found her here? Why?

She plucked the small envelope from its plastic holder with fingers she refused to let tremble. She opened the card, fighting not to let Sandy and the others see her fear as they crowded close.

"You are lovelier than the sunrise," Sandy read over her shoulder. "I am all alone now, but soon we shall be together again, never to be parted." She squealed and grabbed Ike's shoulders. "It certainly sounds like your ex is trying to *un*complicate things."

One of the receptionists faked a swoon. "And how romantic that he sent them here, knowing it was your first day in a new place. That's a man who pays attention."

Ike let the female chatter flow around her, fighting not to shake as a hard knot formed in her stomach. "If you'll excuse me," she said. "I'll be right back."

She bolted for the ladies' room, where she lunged into a stall and threw up.

WILLIAM LOCKED HIS fingers on the edge of his seat within the surveillance vehicle, fighting to keep himself in place for the time being. He wasn't going to jump the gun without a damn good reason and he wasn't yet sure this was enough of a reason.

When she quieted, he said, "The other day, you started to ask me if I'd sent you something." A low burn of anger fisted his gut. "You should've told me you had a stalker."

The monitor in front of him showed the view from the camera near her collarbone. As he watched, the image shifted from the bathroom floor to a toilet stall door, then to the lower half of a bathroom mirror. Ike's hands splashed in the sink, and she rinsed her mouth out, then popped a couple of mints from her purse. Then her fingers came into view, adjusting the camera so he could see her face in the mirror.

She was pale and lovely and fragile-looking as she said, "I didn't think... I don't have a stalker." But her voice shook and her eyes were stark in her face.

"What else did he send? All flowers? Did you keep the notes?" The words *I'm alone now* echoed through William's brain. He wanted to stand and pace, wanted to throw something, but inside the surveillance pod there was barely room to breathe.

"No, I didn't keep the notes." She swallowed hard. "This is the third delivery, all flowers. I got one the day of Zed's funeral. At first..." Her cheeks pinked. "At first I thought they might've been from you. I thought I saw you there."

"I was there," he admitted, "but I sent flowers to his family, not you." He hadn't known the dead man, had barely known Ike, but she'd made a hell of an impression. And given that she'd been drawn into the danger through Max, William had felt compelled to do something, to apologize somehow for having not stopped The Nine.

"What about the second delivery?" he prompted.

"It was sent to my office at Boston General, maybe a month ago. The first card said something about us being together. The second one was a fashion critique."

An ugly feeling congealed in William's gut. "In what way?"

"He—" she faltered, and he saw that she'd gotten the hint in the latest note, as well. Her secret admirer was alone, just as Odin was now alone. "He said I should wear dresses more and take better care of my appearance."

"Did he say why?" William demanded, not liking this one bit.

She shook her head. "No. But I'm wearing a dress now, and he must've followed me…." Tears gathered in her eyes and voice. "Oh, God. If he developed a thing for me during Max's case, then Zed…" She trailed off, looking stricken, unable to finish the thought, unable to process the idea that her lover hadn't been killed in her stead, he'd been killed so she would remain single.

William's gut clenched. "That's it, I'm pulling the plug. Your cover's no longer secure. If you're not in the parking lot in five minutes, I'm coming in after you."

He expected a fight. If anything, his worry increased when she nodded, eyes stark and hollow in her face. "I'm on my way."

IKE FLED FROM THE ladies' room straight down the back stairs. She was shaking in earnest by the time she pushed through the last door to the parking lot, where she saw William waiting for her beside the SUV.

She burst into tears, ran to him and flung herself into his arms.

He caught her close and held on tight as she burrowed in and clutched at his shirt, pressing her hot face to the curve of his neck, simultaneously embarrassed by the outburst and terrified by the concept that she was being stalked by the leader of The Nine.

"Let's get out of here." He hustled her into the SUV and laid rubber getting them out of the parking lot, then wove through the streets, doubling back several times to make sure they weren't being followed. Finally, on the outskirts of the city, he pulled over in a secluded spot beneath an overpass and threw the SUV into park. Then he unbuckled his belt, turned to her and held out a hand. "Come here."

She went willingly, needing the human contact, the connection that told her she was still alive, still free, not locked away and forgotten somewhere small and dark. And perhaps he'd meant just that—a brief embrace, a reassurance that their plan had failed but they were still alive, still determined to take down Odin and any remnants of his organization. But whatever the intent, things changed the moment their bodies aligned.

Heat flared through Ike as she slid her arms around his waist and felt the solid male flesh beneath his T-shirt and jeans. She knew she shouldn't find excitement in the moment but was helpless to fight the sensation as she pressed her face into the hollow of his neck and breathed him in, filling her lungs with the scent of the man who had talked to her in the darkness and who had worried about her.

She'd never found protectiveness sexy before. Now she thought she might begin to understand the pull. She eased away from him and looked up, wondering if the heat and the awful, terrible temptation was all one-sided, and found herself held prisoner in his eyes, which burned with a desire that matched her own.

They met halfway as though they were lovers already, pausing briefly to look in each other's eyes and exhale a hint of breath. And then their lips touched. Held. Parted.

And rationality was lost.

He tasted of fear and frustration. Or maybe those were her emotions as she sank into him, let him sink into her. They kissed and kissed again in long, searching explorations of lip and tongue that spun out endlessly. The windows grew moist and fogged over, and a passing motorist honked, but Ike didn't care as she touched him, stroking whatever part of him she could reach, wishing they were somewhere else, someplace more comfortable.

I want this, she thought—or maybe she said the words aloud, because he shifted the angle of the kiss, delving deeper and freeing a hand to trace her breast through the light fabric of her dress. She arched against his touch, straining to get closer to him in the small confines of the car, then turned her head to nip a delicate path down the side of his neck, where she fastened on and suckled for a moment, eliciting a groan from deep within his chest.

"William," she said, whispering his name, glorying at the feel and taste of him, the rasp of stubble against her cheek and throat and the hard muscles that bunched and flexed at her touch. "Oh, *William.*"

He shuddered, the motion transmitting throughout his big body as he withdrew from her, pulling away to stare down at her, his ribs heaving with great draughts of air, his eyes dark with passion. Then they darkened further as he looked around. "God. We're under a damned bridge."

"Then let's find someplace better," Ike suggested, having no doubt they were on the same page. They needed to scratch the itch or go mad, relieve the tension lest it distract them from their pursuit of Odin.

The very thought of taking William inside her, of unleashing all the raw power promised in his kiss, had Ike's inner muscles clenching on a warm rush of desire and had her heart stuttering ever so slightly on a hitch of nerves. Her previous lovers—and there had been more than she cared to admit—had been good men, strong enough for a no-strings, no-frills relationship. And if none of them had ever progressed to the point of love, none of them had truly hurt when the end came a few weeks or months later.

William was already different. Her feelings for him were already different. Yet even that wasn't enough to dissuade her, because since when did Ike Rombout back down from a challenge?

You're not Ike right now, a small, sly voice whispered. *You're Eleanor.*

William exhaled and pulled even farther away from her. "We should talk."

"Fair enough. I'm a big fan of going in with my eyes open." Ike straightened and tugged at her dress. "Lord knows I've never been shy, so I'll start." She took a deep breath, then let it out slowly, aware that his eyes flicked to her breasts, aware that her nipples peaked beneath his regard. Her blood churned, yearned, as she said, "We can make this work, keep it totally separate from the case. Hell, scratching the itch'll probably help us focus rather than distracting us. I don't know about you, but I'm just about cross-eyed right now. If you don't kiss me in the next minute or so, I'm going to implode."

Tension thrummed through her, collecting in a hard knot at her core, a clench of muscles anticipating his kiss and his touch.

Instead of kissing her, William actually winced. "That wasn't what I was going to say at all."

The icy slap of rejection stung her with unfamiliar venom, seizing her lungs and stealing the oxygen from the air around her. "Then what exactly were you going to say?"

"That I can't do this." The awkward regret in his expression was more painful than a gut punch. "I'm sorry," he said again, wounding her with his pity. "I didn't mean for it to go that far. Hell, I didn't mean for it to get started in the first place. But it needs to stop."

Her lips felt stiff and odd when she said, "Why?"

"Because the woman I'm attracted to doesn't really exist."

WILLIAM'S EXES might've been unanimous in calling him honest to a fault—even to the point of coldness—but he'd always figured it was best to get the tough stuff out there and be done with it. However, when hurt flashed in Ike's eyes for a split second before her expression blanked, he wished he could've taken the words back.

There probably wasn't a better way to say it, but there might have been a better time.

Her movements were stiff as she returned to her seat and buckled her belt, pulling it snug across her breasts. "My bad. I guess I just figured we could enjoy each other rather than driving ourselves crazy thinking about what it might be like." She paused. "And I meant what I said earlier. Thanks for everything you did today, from talking me down in the closet to pulling me out when those flowers came. I appreciate the backup."

"No problem. Just doing my job." He put the SUV into drive, swiped at his window and got them moving again, foot heavy on the accelerator until he consciously eased off, knowing he couldn't outrun the temptation sitting beside him; he'd have to be strong enough to stay focused on his own hook.

"Where are we headed?" she asked, faking calm.

"To the hotel to get our things," William said. "We'll have to assume the whole plan is compromised—we'll ditch the vehicle and find something else to drive, book into a new hotel. I'll call Max and have him get in touch with Kupfer, maybe through Zach Cage. Odin needs to gain control of the adjunct recipe before he goes public, so we'll need to get Kupfer and his people protected 24-7 from now until Friday's press conference." He cut her a look. "I'd love to send you back to Boston, but we both know you wouldn't stay put."

"Meaning?" she asked, voice tight.

"Meaning you're a target, and I don't trust for an instant that you'll be able to keep yourself out of the action. That makes you my problem for the next few days." When anger flared in her eyes alongside something softer and less sure, he glanced away. "Don't look at me like that."

"Like what?"

"Like you're a typical female and I've hurt your feelings." Wincing again at how badly he was managing to put things, he said, "We both know this isn't you, Ike. You're not into dresses or teamwork and you normally dislike the hell out of me. If there's some chemistry going on between us right now, it's just because of the situation."

She looked away and muttered. "I don't dislike you. You've sort of grown on me, like mold or something."

And for a split second she sounded like the Ike he remembered, which just made things worse. He paused, then sighed heavily before honesty compelled him to say, "Same goes, and that's an even bigger problem. You see—" He broke off as they reached their hotel. "Come on. We need to keep moving."

They climbed out of the SUV and entered the hotel together, with William staying slightly behind and to the right of her, tense and ready to react if Odin had an ambush in place. *Soon we'll be together.* That sounded more like a promise than a threat, and the thought of either had him strung tight.

Hell, he acknowledged inwardly, there was nothing about this situation that didn't have him wired.

Once they were headed to their rooms with no sign of an ambush, he said, "I was on a job once that went real bad real fast and a female agent died. I'm not about to let that happen again."

She sent him a look that was pure Ike beneath the soft hair and makeup. "Was she the only fellow agent you ever saw die?"

"Her name was Sharilee and unfortunately, no, she wasn't the only agent I've ever seen die."

"Did you love her?"

Alarm bells went off in William's head, but he said, "No. I knew her to chat with, nothing more."

"Then you're stuck on her being a woman," Ike said flatly. "That's insulting."

"It's life," he argued. "We live in a society where men are raised to respect women. A man can hit another man, but he's an abusive jerk if he hits a woman." He held up a hand. "I'm not saying that's wrong, it's the way it should be. But given that, how can you expect us to forget your sex under other circumstances?"

"That's your problem, not mine. I didn't ask you to look out for me."

"Max did."

"He doesn't have the right," she said levelly as the elevator let them out on their floor. "If I want to put my life in danger, that's my choice. It's my life, and nobody can tell me what to do with it."

For a second he thought he caught an echo of loneliness in the statement, which had him softening his immediate response. "Max is your friend, Ike. He wants to see you come out of this alive. So do I."

The last three words came out of nowhere, surprising him with their truth.

Uncertainty flickered in her eyes, but

then her expression hardened. "I don't intend to commit suicide, but nor do I intend to hide while the menfolk take care of Odin. I owe Zed, and Lukas Kupfer is a good man with a noble goal. Odin is going down, and I intend to be there."

Because he could relate even if he didn't agree, William tipped his head as he keyed them into his room. "Then we're at an impasse."

Knowing it was almost a relief, since it gave him another reason to stay away.

She lifted one shoulder. "That's nothing new." But as she opened the connecting door between their rooms and started gathering lightweight computer bags, she said with almost forced casualness, "Guess that means no more kissing, huh?"

"I think we both know that was a mistake we shouldn't repeat. Besides, you can ditch the disguise now. Once you're back to normal, it shouldn't be an issue."

The insult was deliberate, and he knew damn well he deserved it when she slammed the connecting door in his face. He stood there a moment, waiting for the relief, for the knowledge that he'd done what he'd needed to do for her safety, for his own sanity.

All he found was disappointment and a faint suspicion that he'd done it more for his own good than hers.

Chapter Eight

Ike was a professional, so she kept it together while they checked out of one hotel and checked into another equally generic hotel on the other side of Springfield. She allowed nothing but business in her voice when she called Max and then Zach Cage, arranging for HFH to contact Lukas Kupfer, explain the situation and send protection. And she held her cool as she set up Tom, Dick and Harry in her new hotel room and changed out of the dress, replacing it with a pair of jeans and a pale pink sweatshirt, which had been Stephen's idea of Eleanor-goes-casual.

But inwardly she was a mess, as the day's event collapsed onto her in a big, tumultuous blob of unhappiness that included

Odin's flowers, her claustrophobia attack and William's kiss, and then culminated in the knowledge that he'd been kissing Eleanor. He was attracted to the disguise, not her.

Rage swirled inside her, the cumulative fury of a lifetime worth of being second best, of being a workout buddy rather than a woman, a quick fling rather than a heartbreaker. But instead of showing the hurt, she held herself aloof, hiding behind the shell she'd perfected long ago, when they'd buried her brother and she'd stood at the gravesite a half dozen paces from her parents, who hadn't needed or wanted to include her in their grief.

Feeling that same sharp hurt now and damning whatever of Eleanor's vulnerability had leaked into her, she raised her voice so William could hear her in his adjoining room. "I'm online. Who should I start with—Grosskill or Johnson and Leon?"

She might not like William very much at the moment, but that didn't change the fact that he was a trained agent. It would be stupid for her not to use the resources she had at hand, and people rarely accused her of stupidity. Other faults, perhaps, but not stupidity.

He appeared in the doorway, crossed the room and leaned over her, close enough that she had to grit her teeth and ignore the flare of heat. Even knowing he'd been kissing Eleanor didn't dampen the memory of how his body had pressed solidly against hers and how he'd caressed her with lazy, devastating skill.

She'd been too long without a man, that was all, Ike assured herself. She just needed to blow off some steam. It wasn't about William.

And if that rang faintly false, she was the only one to know it.

"Grosskill's a bad agent, but he's not an idiot," William said grudgingly. "His involvement will be buried seriously deep. Better start with the fourth floor lab and see if you can get any dirt on Johnson or Leon."

"Will do." Ike cracked her knuckles and bent to the task, more relieved than she cared to admit to be back at her keyboards, working programs that knew nothing of lust or emotion.

She called up basic Internet searches on Tom, then used a couple of her long-established back-door entry programs to sneak Dick and Harry into databases at the FDA and National Institute of Health. She remained aware of William still leaning over her and was conscious of the faint tickle of his breath against the back of her neck. Finally she glanced over at him. "Was there something else?"

His face was very close to hers, almost close enough to kiss, until he straightened away from her and stuck his hands in the pockets of his jeans. "I'm sorry about what I said before. You know, about liking Eleanor better."

Ike's banked irritation resurfaced with a snap. "Don't apologize for telling the truth."

He nodded and backed up a few steps but didn't leave. "What are you doing for dinner?"

She turned back to the computers so he

couldn't see how uncomfortable she was becoming with the conversation and with his presence in her hotel room. "Room service. Or, if you're going out, you can grab me something." She shot him a look. "I'll stay put tonight. Promise."

He nodded as though he'd expected nothing less. "Max will be here in the morning. You'll have something for us by then?"

"That I can guarantee." She didn't know what, but she'd damn well have something. She was many things, but she was no quitter.

IN FACT, BY THE TIME the next morning rolled around and the three of them met in William's room, she had a great deal more than something. She had Dominic Firenzetti.

"It wasn't easy," she said, "but I found him. After Kupfer caught him siphoning their grant money, he changed his name to Daniel Francona, but facial recognition software on a film clip confirmed the match. These days he's an 'entrepreneur—'" she used her fingers to emphasize the quote marks "—with home bases in L.A. and Washington, D.C. It looks like he's got interests in a bunch of scientific fields, including plastic surgery and gene therapy." She shot Max a look. "Sound familiar?"

He nodded. "Sure does." The Nine had targeted Raine's sex enhancement drug because it improved the self-esteem of its users, threatening a sharp decline in cosmetic surgery procedures. Add that to Firenzetti/Francona's apparent escape from prosecution and his rise to power, and they had good evidence for him being a member of The Nine or at least a beneficiary of their largesse.

She handed each man a brief printout containing stats and photographs. "He wasn't on the plane that crashed in the Catskills, which suggests he's probably a one-off supporter of The Nine rather than a member."

William glanced at the printout, then back at her. "You don't think he's Odin?"

"No, I don't, but that's just my gut check, and I'm working on limited information, so take it for what it's worth."

She expected him to dismiss her instinct. Instead he said, "I'd tend to agree. No offense, but I don't think we're going to find our mastermind online."

"Exactly. Which is why I think we should have a look around the fourth floor, maybe even tonight. If nothing else, maybe we can find some evidence connecting Grosskill to the Markham Institute. That might be enough to get someone higher up in the Bureau to pay attention."

"What have you got on Johnson and Leon?" Max asked, setting aside the printout. "Anything to suggest they've got it in for Kupfer? If so, that could be the weak link Odin is planning to exploit tomorrow."

Tomorrow, Ike thought, realizing it was already Thursday. They were almost out of time. According to Max, Kupfer had accepted protection but had refused to change the day or location of the press conference. He was too familiar with the urban legend of The Nine to believe that they really existed.

"I didn't find anything unusual on either of the scientists on the fourth floor," she admitted. "They've published a bunch of articles on gene therapy in the middle-tier journals, even had Kupfer as a contributing author on a couple of them. They look legit." She paused, then said, "To be honest, that fourth floor felt seriously understaffed, like everyone had been given the day off. They haven't left completely, because the freezers and cryo chambers out in the hall are still up and running. But I almost wonder if one or both of the primary investigators are getting ready to jump ship...perhaps to a cushy industrial job?"

"Certainly sounds possible," William agreed. "Question is, how are they connected to Firenzetti/Francona, and what the hell was Grosskill doing there?" He rose. "I'm going over to talk to Kupfer."

Ike stood, as well. "I'm going with you." She held up a hand to forestall his automatic denial. "Kupfer and I have a rapport. He'll talk to me more easily."

William snorted. "He'll be ticked that you lied to him."

"I can deal with that." She held his gaze and said, "I can help." They both knew she was really saying, *I'm part of this. Don't shut me out just because I'm a woman.*

Finally he nodded, reluctance etched in the tense set of his shoulders. "Fine, have it your way. We leave in ten minutes."

WILLIAM HALF HOPED Ike would choose to wear her normal, unrelieved tight black clothes to their meeting, chucking the disguise and returning to her regular self. Instead she appeared wearing flowing slacks in dark navy, along with a clingy white top and a neatly zipped navy jacket. The overall effect should have been businesslike. It failed.

She tipped her head. "Something wrong?"

Yes, everything was wrong. They were on an op and they needed to stay focused on that op. She couldn't know how far his thoughts threatened to wander now that he'd tasted her or how he'd found himself sitting up long into the previous night worrying not just because she was his responsibility but because she was who and what she was, a beautiful, desirable—

Whoa, he thought desperately. *Where did that come from?* And how much of it was Ike, how much Eleanor? Either way, he needed to keep it in perspective—this was an op, not a weekend holiday. If he didn't focus, he was going to make mistakes. If he made mistakes, she could suffer the consequences.

And that would make him no better than Michael Grosskill.

So he shook his head and said firmly, "No problem at all. Let's go."

On the short ride to the Markham Institute, silence pervaded their new vehicle, a silver econobox he'd rented under one of the several fake identities he and Max each kept in their emergency kits along with cash and spare weapons.

There was no sign of pursuit during the drive, and there was no sign of surveillance as they walked across the parking lot to Kupfer's building, but William kept his vigilance high.

If Odin wanted Ike for himself, he'd have to get through William first.

Ike keyed them through to the fifth floor

and led him into the lab lobby, stopping at the sight of a cheerful-looking blond woman standing beside a wheelchair-bound boy. William recognized the blonde as Kupfer's head tech, Sandy. The boy was light-haired and blue-eyed. His bone structure was that of a handsome teen, but his skin was sallow and he was painfully gaunt. His stick-thin legs were strapped in place, their weakness a stark contrast to his muscled arms.

Sandy's eyes lit. "Eleanor!" Then her expression darkened to concern and her gaze flicked to William and back. "We were worried when you disappeared yesterday. I take it the flowers weren't good news?" She grimaced. "I'm sorry we were being so silly about the delivery. We thought…" She trailed off and gestured helplessly.

"It's okay," Ike said, voice strangely husky. "Who's this?"

"This is Jeremy Talbott." The tech moved closer to the wheelchair. "He helps Dr. Kupfer with experiments now and then."

"I donate blood every few months," the

young man elaborated. "Doc lets me spin the samples and sometimes I help prep the experiments. I've got a rare mutation in the dystrophin gene, and Doc is trying to come up with a new test."

"I'm going to have to postpone until next week," a new voice said, drawing William's attention to the lab doorway, where Kupfer stood, white-coated and grim-faced. He nodded to Sandy. "His transport is waiting downstairs. Something's come up that I need to take care of immediately. I'm closing the lab for the rest of the day and tomorrow morning. We'll reopen after the press conference."

"Um…okay." Sandy frowned and looked from Kupfer to the others and back. "Is there anything I can do to help?"

Kupfer smiled, but the expression didn't reach his eyes. "Enjoy the half day off and I'll see you tomorrow afternoon." Then he turned to William and Ike and gestured them into his office. "This way."

Inside the small, cluttered room, William stood near the doorway while Ike took the single visitor's chair. Only it wasn't really

Ike in the chair, it was Eleanor in a trim navy outfit and careful makeup, with her long hair left free to cascade down her slim back.

Only that wasn't right either, William realized with a start. Eleanor didn't exist, she was a made-up cover story. Oddly, though, it seemed as though the person sitting opposite Kupfer was a mix of the two women. Ike's wit and edge shone in her eyes, but the hair and makeup softened the effect, making her seem determined rather than intimidating. Resolute rather than aggressive.

"I owe you an apology," she said to Kupfer without preamble.

He grimaced. "I spoke to Zach Cage at length. He says you're a computer hacker. Bravo on your acting abilities, because you had me convinced that not only were you a scientist but that you understood the importance of my work."

Ike flinched but said, "You weren't wrong. I did my postgrad work in a lab like yours. And I understand more than you'd think."

Kupfer didn't look convinced or cooperative. "You're too young to have lost a child to DMD."

She shook her head. "My brother had Down syndrome. He died when he was fifteen." She glanced up at William, and he saw something move in her eyes before she focused on Kupfer and said, "My family fell apart afterward, just like yours, and a big chunk of it was my fault."

IKE WAS AWARE OF THE speculation in Kupfer's eyes, but it was William she focused on when he took a half-step toward her, eyes dark.

"Don't." She held up a hand. "Don't pity me. Or him. Donny was…" She paused, remembering his laugh. "He was perfect. A gift. He deserved better than a sister like me." She'd never said those words aloud before, though she'd repeated them often in her heart. Getting them out there now was both freeing and depressing, and her heart hitched slightly when she said, "By the time he was three, he'd had six operations, fixing heart problems and a malformation in his digestive tract. My father's insurance plan wasn't that good, and when Donny was ten, my mother had to get a job to help pay for the next cardiac surgery." She stared down at the darkening streets, watching the traffic. "I babysat. At first I hated it. Frankly, until then I'd spent as little time as possible with him, but the little guy grew on me, fast. He was…"

She trailed off, trying to find the words, talking to herself now as much as to the others. "He was fun. He had a great sense of humor, even when he wasn't feeling well. He loved baseball and animals." And for some reason, he'd loved her, as well. Never mind that she was too tall and thin, that she hadn't grown breasts like the other girls and didn't care about clothes and music the way they did.

Her parents had urged her to fit in and make friends. Donny had loved her just the way she was.

"What happened?" Kupfer asked.

"He got sick again, too sick for them to operate. They needed to get him stabilized first, and he wound up staying in the hospital. Two, three weeks he was there without much change. My parents were always either at work or at the hospital with him. I…I got fed up. They missed something of mine." She shook her head. "I can't even remember what now—maybe a science fair or something, it doesn't really matter—but I'd convinced myself it was the most important thing in the world. I lost my temper and shouted at my mother when she called me from the hospital, then I ran upstairs and locked myself in the linen closet, thinking…" She trailed off and shook her head. "Hell, I don't know what I was thinking—probably that she'd be scared when she rushed home to make sure I was okay and couldn't find me. Only she didn't come home. I sat in there for hours, waiting, getting madder and madder, until I finally cried myself to sleep."

She felt William approach, felt the good, warm weight of his hand on her shoulder. She knew she should shake him off, that he wouldn't have offered the gesture if she'd been dressed in her normal clothes, if they'd been under normal circumstances. But she didn't, instead drawing comfort from him when she continued. "They didn't come home until the next day, and my mother yelled at me when she found me in the closet." Ike remembered the words *spoiled, selfish brat* and couldn't argue. "Donny's heart had given out. He was fifteen years old."

William's fingers tightened on her shoulder. "And you were, what, sixteen? Practically a kid. Give yourself a break."

"I didn't say goodbye. After we buried him…" She broke off and swallowed hard. "After, my parents and I barely spoke for the next couple of years, until I went off to college. I never went back." A tear broke free and trickled down her cheek, but she let it lie in an almost calculating move as she turned to Kupfer. "So, yeah, I understand why you've dedicated your life to DMD research. And, trust me, I understand why this press conference is important to you and to kids like Jeremy out there. So please. Let us help you."

KUPFER'S EYES reflected surprise, but he inclined his head. "Then maybe I wasn't as wrong as I thought." He flicked a glance at William. "Are you Vasek or Caine?"

"William Caine. We'd like to ask you a few questions about your former partner, Dominic Firenzetti, and about the researchers on the fourth floor of this building."

But even as William led Kupfer through the questions, his mind was split, with one part of him focused on the interview and one part of him trying to assimilate the information Ike had just given him.

It explained more than she probably knew.

"Dominic was brilliant," Kupfer said. "He was—or rather is—far smarter than I, though it took me some time to realize that, since he focused many of his energies on things other than our research."

"When did that change?" Ike asked. "When did he become interested in the work?"

Kupfer frowned. "I'd say about six months before I discovered he was embezzling the grant money. He became friends with an investor. Something Smith. After that, suddenly Dominic was in the lab every day, sometimes on weekends, totally focused on the gene therapy vector we were building at the time."

That got William's attention. The name wouldn't get them far, even with Ike's undeniable talents, but it was a start. "Do you think this Smith had something to do with the turnaround?"

"Most likely." Kupfer plucked the stuffed toy dog from his desk and tossed it from hand to hand in what looked like a habitual gesture, revealing a small framed picture that had been hidden behind the dog. It showed the same blond woman, only without the boy, making William think Lucille Kupfer wasn't as much of an ex-wife as the eight-year-old divorce would suggest.

Kupfer continued, "When Dominic left, he took some of his work with him—the sequences to a couple of viral constructs and a few other things. To be honest, I didn't make a big deal of it. I was just happy to have him out of the lab with relatively little drama. But the other day when Miss Roth—" He caught himself. "Miss Rombout drew my attention to his name, I realized the constructs he took contain some of the elements in the adjunct."

"So maybe Dominic knew he was onto something, and this Smith paid him to steal it, thinking it was closer to completion than it really was," Ike suggested.

William shot her a look and a subtle head shake. True, they were protecting Kupfer, but that didn't mean the researcher was completely above reproach. It didn't pay to share anything more than absolutely necessary. Which is why, when William brought the interview to a close after learning very little about Drs. Johnson and Leon, he didn't ask permission to plant a small audio bug in Kupfer's office. He just did it.

IKE SPENT THE remainder of that day and into the evening holed up in her hotel room. Not because she was following Max and William's orders to stay out of sight but because she wasn't in the mood for people. She felt like a stranger inside her own skin. She was reacting rather than acting, and that wasn't like her at all.

Worse, she couldn't get William's voice out of her head. Even though the earpiece, wire and camera were gone, along with the surveillance vehicle, she kept hearing his whispered comments in her mind, kept feeling the shimmer of his heat on her lips.

He'd gotten under her skin. She didn't know exactly how or when, but he'd snuck past her defenses and become important. And that was a problem because they were teammates on opposite sides of an issue. He wanted her locked away until Odin was brought to justice. Too bad, though, because she intended to be there when the snake went down—hell, she intended to be the one with a foot across his throat. That put her and William directly at odds. Never mind that he wanted a woman who didn't exist.

As if on cue, a quiet knock drew her attention to the hallway door, sending a jolt of heat through her system. Still wearing the navy outfit she'd chosen for their lab visit, she crossed the room and opened the door.

It wasn't William. It was Max.

"Oh," she said, far more disappointed than she should have been. "Hey."

"Want to grab some dinner?"

She glanced at her watch and was surprised to see that it was well past suppertime. Even more surprising, she wasn't particularly hungry, for food or company. "No, thanks. I'm going to keep pounding the info superhighway. There're only about a billion people named Smith to choose from. And besides, tomorrow's going to be a big day." They planned to be in place several hours before the press conference, along with the two HFH operatives Zach Cage had sent to protect Kupfer.

Max hesitated, looking at her long and hard before he nodded. "Okay. See you in the morning."

She closed the door on him, then pressed her ear to the panel. He stood for a moment before he turned and headed down the hall. His reluctance to leave her, coupled with the furtive sounds now coming from William's room next door, only served to confirm her suspicion.

The menfolk thought they were putting one over on her. Well, she'd show them.

She yanked open her suitcase and dug down to the single familiar outfit she'd brought with her. Feeling a buzz just beneath her skin, she stripped out of conservative navy and pulled on basic black. The dark jeans slid on like an old friend, as did the black turtleneck and short biker jacket. Her feet almost wept with relief the moment she pulled on her boots, and when she stood and inhaled, she felt almost normal for the first time in a week.

Then she got a look at herself in the mirror and cringed because the woman who stared back at her remained a stranger. The clothes were right, but her hair was long and light, too close to her natural shade for comfort, and her face was skillfully made up with blush and lip gloss that was far too soft for the hard-edged outfit.

She looked more like a fake now than she had while wearing a dress.

"Hell," she muttered and dived into Eleanor's makeup bag for something that would make the Mary Sue in the mirror disappear.

She was tempted to cut off the hair extensions, but she didn't have enough time, so she settled for pulling her long hair back in a tight ponytail. Then she scrubbed off the makeup and went with her usual swipe of mascara, wishing it were black rather than medium brown.

That helped matters, but her face still looked naked, so she sucked it up and applied a bit of Eleanor's darkest lip gloss.

"Not bad," she said and watched the woman in the mirror shape the words with painted lips. "Just one more accessory."

She popped the false bottom on the suitcase and pulled out a small .22, along with a wallet containing an ID, credit cards and a permit to carry concealed, all in the name Ike Rombout. Checking the safety and clip, she tucked the gun in the small of her back, beneath the biker jacket, and jammed the paperwork in a pocket.

Armed and dangerous, she strode to the connecting door and knocked, primed for a fight. There was a pause before the door opened to reveal William, wearing dark clothes and a resigned expression.

Ike planted herself squarely in front of him and lifted her chin. "Either I go with you or I follow you. Your choice."

He didn't bother to pretend he wasn't headed for the Markham Institute to look around the fourth floor. He gave her a long look up and down, and she wasn't sure how to interpret the change in his eyes before he said flatly, "No. You're not coming with me and you're not following me. I'm not letting you get yourself killed on my watch."

"Nobody asked you to watch me." She held up a hand when he would've contradicted her. "Yes, I'm sure Max made you my protector, but as I believe I've said before, he doesn't have the right to decide what I'm allowed to do and what I'm not. You don't have the right. And Zach Cage might technically be my boss, but that doesn't even give him the right to control me."

This time his expression was a snap to read, because his frustration was a mirror of her own. He sighed heavily. "I don't want to control you, Ike."

Sure you do, she thought. *That's what men do.* But aloud she said, "Then let me come with you. I can help."

"You'll distract me. I'd be so worried about looking after you that I wouldn't be able to concentrate on the job."

She shrugged. "That's your problem, not mine." She gestured down at her black pants. "See? No dress. Just think of me as one of the guys."

He bit back a bark of laughter and then stepped in and leaned down until they were practically nose to nose. "Let's get one thing straight. Even when you're at your most annoying, I've never mistaken you for a man."

This time when the heat flared it didn't die down. Instead kindling a traitorous warmth deep inside her, one that reflected the growing spark in his eyes. *I want you,* it said, *but I won't accept you as an equal.*

Too bad, Ike thought, because that kind of wanting wasn't enough for her. And though she wasn't sure where the thought had come from, it fit in a way her skin, her new hair and her old clothes didn't.

Not stopping to absorb the realization, she said, "Why can't you see that we're both doing this for the same reason? You feel responsible for Sharilee's death, so you're determined to protect me. Zed died because of me, so I'm determined to help you bring Odin down. It's the same. We're the same."

"I'm not trying to keep you alive because of what happened to Sharilee," he said quietly. "Maybe I was at first. But now I'm worried about you because I think the world would be a poorer place without you in it."

That brought Ike to a stuttering halt and punched a fist beneath her heart. She swallowed hard, more affected than she ought to have been when she prided herself on not needing anyone's approval but her own.

She stared at William, who was closer than she'd thought, so close she could feel the heat of his body against her skin. His eyes held silent entreaty. *Do this for me, please.* But she couldn't. She just couldn't.

"Thanks," she said, still shaken by the

idea that he could like her for who she was, then slowly realizing that he didn't. He liked the idea of her but couldn't handle the reality, which was that she wouldn't stay in his shadow, no matter the circumstance. So she stepped away from him, away from the tempting warmth and the promise of a sanctuary that came with conditions. "I appreciate the thought more than you can know. But that doesn't change anything. I want to do this, William. I need to do it. So you choose—am I going with you or am I going on my own?"

He stared at her for a long moment, so long she thought the answer would be no. Then he cursed and turned away, saying over his shoulder, "Have it your way. Just don't slow me down."

Chapter Nine

Not only did she not slow him down, William was forced to admit, she sped things up by bringing him directly to a rear stairwell door he hadn't seen before.

At his inquiring look, she shrugged and said, "I pulled the schematics. Trust me, I was going in with or without you tonight."

There was no sign of surveillance, no alarm as they slipped into the stairwell and climbed to the fourth floor. Granted, the Markham Institute wasn't exactly high on the security scale, but Odin was nothing if not thorough. If there was something to protect on the fourth floor, it would've been protected. The lack of response bothered William, making him think they were on a wild goose chase.

Or walking straight into a trap.

"Wait," he said once she'd bypassed the keypad and opened the door to the fourth floor. "Let me go first."

He expected an argument. She surprised him by stepping back.

Drawing his weapon, William slipped through the door and into a darkened hallway, which was lit only by emergency lights that gleamed small pools of brightness on the waxed floor. The air smelled faintly stale, but that might've been his imagination.

He waited a beat but didn't hear anything above the faint hum of blowers and automated machinery. Gesturing for Ike to follow, he stepped into the hallway and let the door close and latch, then indicated that she should lead. If she'd memorized the schematics for the building, she'd know where the offices were located, and that would be the best place to start.

Moments later they were inside a roomy office with *Dr. Minor J. Johnson* stenciled on the door.

Ike took a seat at the neat-looking desk,

pulled the computer keyboard into position and glanced up at him. "What do you think?"

He briefly debated the wisdom of accessing the institute's intranet, then gave her a go-ahead gesture. "If they didn't notice us breaking in, they're not likely to log the computer access until business hours tomorrow, and by that time it'll be pretty much over one way or the other." Either Odin would have made his move and been captured or they'd be back to square negative one, with precious few leads and no idea as to his next target.

William refused to consider the third possibility—that Odin would strike and escape—because based on his note Kupfer wasn't the only target now. Ike was in danger, too, and William didn't intend to let the bastard hurt her.

She'd made it clear that she didn't want to be his responsibility, but that was too bad, because somewhere along the line she'd become exactly that. He wasn't sure when or how she'd sneaked past his defenses, but there she was, lodged in a place that had been closed off for a long time, longer perhaps than he'd even been aware.

Whether she liked it or not, he intended to keep her safe—or die trying.

"Get going." She made a shooing motion, then turned back to the computer. "I'll need ten, maybe fifteen minutes if I'm going to be sure I don't leave tracks."

"You've got ten," he said, feeling the seconds tick beneath his skin. The lack of an alarm suggested there was no manned security in place, but could be a remote system to call the cops in the event of a break-in.

He didn't intend to stick around long enough to find out. With Grosskill somehow involved, they couldn't even trust the local police.

Though a deep-seated masculine instinct told William to stay with Ike, logic and necessity sent him back out into the lab lobby. He rifled the receptionist's desk and flipped through her day planner, finding nothing more incriminating than a reminder of a two-o'clock meeting with

"G," which might or might not refer to Grosskill. Then he moved into the second large office, which belonged to Dr. Karma Leon. The trash can beneath the desk was empty, but when William pulled it out of the kneehole, he found a small collection of wadded-up Post-its jammed behind the can. A quick scan yielded two arrow-bearing Sign Here notes and a few blank Post-its. Alone, the findings were nothing he could build a case on, but he made note of the arrows, which suggested an official document.

A licensing contract with the mysterious Smith? Maybe, maybe not. Still nothing concrete, and the minutes were ticking down on his estimated safety zone, so he headed for the lab itself. He had his hand on the airlock door handle when he heard Ike's low cry of triumph.

He was at her side in an instant, leaning over to peer past her shoulder at the computer screen. "What've you got?"

"More on Firenzetti." She keyed in a command, and a printer in the corner of the room began churning out pages. "Johnson

had a meeting with him two weeks ago."
She shot him a look. "He keeps showing
up. Makes me start to think he might be our
guy after all."

William's wrist unit chimed faintly, signaling the end of their ten minutes. "Nice
work. Grab your papers and let's get out of
here."

He couldn't have said why, but he was
convinced their time was running out. Instincts flared to life, old survival tactics he
hadn't used since his time undercover in the
Trehern operation, old fighting patterns he'd
consciously tried to forget since his years in
the military, when the things his sensei had
thought beautiful had been turned violent
and corrupt in the name of survival.

"You find anything?" she asked as she
folded the pages and tucked them into her
waistband next to the pistol she'd concealed
beneath her short black jacket.

"Only that everything seems to have
ground to a halt Tuesday afternoon," he
said. "There's nothing dated after that
point. It's like the whole lab staff suddenly
stood up and walked out."

He didn't bother voicing the other possibility—that Odin had killed them in order to control floor space very near the Kupfer lab. But when Ike passed him on her way out of Johnson's office, her tight expression spoke volumes, making him want to hold her and tell her everything would be okay.

He didn't, though, because he didn't have the right and because they both knew it would be an empty promise. They were working on partial information, doing the best they could without official backup. Worse, it appeared they were quite likely working *against* an official response, if Grosskill's involvement was anything to go by.

They knew to be on the lookout for Firenzetti, but was that going to be enough to help them in the next few hours? William didn't think so as he followed Ike down the stairs. Sure, he could give the name to Grosskill's higher-ups, but with no evidence and no assurance that those same higher-ups weren't involved, it would be like spitting on a bonfire. Useless.

Without major evidence, it came right

down to the bare bones—their best bet was staking out the press conference.

When they hit the bottom floor, Ike grabbed the outer door handle and glanced at him, waiting for his go-ahead. He pushed past her. "I'll take point."

He eased open the door and looked around. The parking lot looked exactly the same as it had when they arrived—deserted blacktop lit in places by cones of orangey sodium light. It had started raining while they were inside, slicking the pavement and lending a chilly haze to the air.

Seeing nothing unexpected, William nodded. "We're good. Come on."

He led the way across the parking lot, bound for the corner where they'd scaled a chain-link fence from a nearby cross street rather than passing the security cameras at the main gate. Ike pulled herself over the fence without waiting for his assist, dropping down lightly on the other side, where an alley opened onto the street near where they'd parked their rented car.

William was halfway up the chain link when a crack of gunfire split the night.

"Hurry!" Ike shouted. She whipped out her .22, spun and returned fire.

William launched himself up and over the fence, landing hard. "Come on!"

He grabbed her arm and pulled her across the alley, where a door was set into the wall of a featureless gray building. He kicked the door hard, heard the lock mechanism give slightly and kicked again, then hit the slab as hard as he could with his shoulder. The door gave way, spitting them into a cavernous space. It took William a moment to register the smell of oil and the big, dark bulks of vehicles. A mechanic's garage.

"There! The door!" Ike tugged him toward the far side of the building. "Hurry!"

The sound of footsteps approaching from behind spurred him on. He ran across the garage floor, popped the lock on the front door and hurled it open.

Then he dragged Ike back into the garage. If the bastard had set up one ambush, no doubt he'd set up a second.

"This way." He pulled her around a corner

and down a short hallway as their pursuers entered the garage, feet clattering on the cement floor. "Come on." He urged her deeper into a mazelike series of cubicles hung with pictures of cars and women, the details barely visible in the low illumination of emergency lights.

There, William froze and listened. He heard a low-voiced conversation, and then two sets of footsteps heading out the front, through the door he'd left open. Ike stirred as though to move away, but he tightened his grip and shook his head quickly, mouthing, *Stop. Listen.*

Sure enough, thirty seconds later they heard motion in the outer room, then the sound of a car door squeaking open and shut. At least one of their attackers had stayed behind, maybe more.

William glanced around, and his eyes lit on a series of tall lockers, most of which stood half-open and empty, a few hung with spare jackets and overalls.

Footsteps squeaked on the cement, drawing nearer.

William felt Ike tense beside him. Knowing there was no better answer, he bent down and whispered, "I'm sorry."

She mouthed, *For what?*

"This." As the measured footsteps drew nearer still, he grabbed her, spun her so they were plastered front to front, and walked them into one of the lockers.

Then he shut the door, cutting out the light.

She went board-stiff against him. "You're okay," he whispered almost soundlessly. "I'm here. I've got you."

When she didn't respond, he wrapped his arms around her, urging her away from the door, closer to his body, hoping his touch would ease her fear.

The action had the exact opposite effect on his own body, which heated as she fit tight against him, lining up hard to soft, heat to heat.

She made a wordless sound of protest, though he wasn't sure if she was fighting him or the darkness that surrounded them.

"Hush," he whispered in her ear, barely a breath of sound as the footsteps approached.

Through the slats in the metal cabinet door William could see a male figure in black-on-black livery. One of Odin's bodyguards.

Under other circumstances, he would've taken the guy on, but with Ike in there with him, that wasn't an option. He'd made the wrong choice once before and wasn't taking that risk again.

Besides, he had a more immediate problem, he realized as she began to shake against him, trembling with growing panic. She clutched at his shirt, grabbing on as though he were her lifeline. He tightened his hold, trying to wrap himself around her, trying to give her the illusion of safety, though they were anything but safe.

He heard her breaths come quickly, felt her heartbeat pound against his flesh.

More car doors slammed, and male voices called to each other.

"You find them?" one called.

"Nope," another answered. "Keep looking. I don't think they went out the front."

Ike's trembling increased until William could feel the motion in his very core, transmitted through flesh and bone. A faint sound escaped from her and was quickly muffled, but it sounded as loud as a shout to his ears.

Sh, he wanted to say but didn't dare. *You're okay. I've got you. I promise I won't let anything happen to you.*

Since he couldn't say the words, he did the next best thing, the thing he'd been thinking of all day or perhaps for far longer than that. He bent down and gathered her even closer so her flesh was pressed hard against his, their hearts beat in tandem and they breathed the same air.

And he kissed her.

It was the same as before, all sharp flavor and hot promise. Except it was different because this time he wasn't kissing Eleanor. He was kissing Ike.

THERE WAS NO MOMENT of hesitation, no gentle question. One minute she was stuck in her own head, trying not to break and scream as the darkness pressed in, suffocating her. In the next, William was kissing her as though they were lovers already, as though he knew exactly where to touch her and how and had the absolute right to do it.

His lips claimed hers forcefully, expertly, and the way they were plastered together in the tiny space left no doubt of his arousal. His tongue played across her lips, demanding access, and when she opened her mouth in shock, he swept inside to claim a deeper kiss, one that sent her senses spinning and put her outside herself.

The tiny cabinet disappeared. The armed thugs outside disappeared. In that instant there was only the man pressed against her, making love to her with his mouth.

He framed her face between his big hands and concentrated on her lips, as if instinctively knowing she didn't like to be held too tight, that she liked to be free to move away if she wished. Only there was no thought of that as she pressed closer to him, catching a moan before it was born, holding onto the sensations that piled one atop the other.

He tasted of the same frustration that

rode her, had ridden her for days now, maybe longer.

Sharp, edgy need flooded her, flooring her with the burn of desire and a gut-clenching lust that demanded release. And not just any release but completion with this man—the pounding, gut-churning, raw-edged sex his kiss promised.

"Hey," a loud male voice said suddenly, sounding as though it came from mere feet away. "Did you two check the offices back here?"

There was a loud banging as first one cabinet was opened and then the next. Heat went to ice in an instant in Ike's body as the door to their hiding spot was yanked open and a bright flashlight beam pierced the darkness. "Got 'em!" a voice yelled.

Then William exploded from the cabinet in a blur of muscle and motion, and the other man's yell became a scream. Ike could barely follow William's moves as he caught the black-clad bodyguard by the throat and chest, flipped the guy and had him on the ground between one heartbeat and the next.

She stood, shocked by the speed and the violence.

The guy twitched once, then went still, but William was already gone, flashing across the room to take on two other assailants who burst into the room at a dead run, weapons drawn.

Ike pulled her .22, but William didn't need her weapon or even his own. Without slackening pace, he grabbed one man and slammed him into the other. Gunfire echoed in the open space, bullets ricocheting as the men fired wildly. Ike screamed and backpedaled to the cabinet, taking shelter behind one of the open locker doors.

William spun and grabbed one of the men by the throat. There was an audible click and the guy went limp. His weapon clattered free when he dropped to the floor, but William didn't care. He grabbed the other guy, spun him and slammed him into the door frame headfirst. He went down hard, leaving William standing in the center of the room, breathing hard, seeming unhurt.

But not untouched, Ike decided when he turned and looked at her, his eyes dark and wild. Whatever he'd done just now, whatever place inside him channeled that level of fighting prowess, it wasn't a place he wanted to be.

He'd gone there for her, she realized on a punch of emotion. He'd become someone he didn't want to be in order to make sure she wouldn't get hurt.

She took a step away from the cabinet and held out her hand. "William—"

Voices shouted from the other room, and something metal overturned with a clatter. William spun toward the sound and bared his teeth, flexing his fingers in preparation for another battle. But instead of racing out to meet the attack, he backpedaled two steps, planting himself square in the center of the office.

When a shadowy figure appeared in the doorway, he lowered his head and growled, "If you want her, you'll have to go through me, you bastard."

The words speared through Ike, frightening her with the intensity of her reaction, the intensity of her fear when the figure raised one hand and she realized he could shoot William where he stood and all the fighting arts in the world couldn't outstrip a bullet.

Then the other man stepped into the light, and sharp relief flooded through her at the sight of Max, hands raised to show peaceful intent. "Chill, partner. It's me, and I've got some of Springfield's finest with me, rounding up the others. Don't worry, I've got Cage leaning on the state police. We'll be able to hold them for a few days on weapons charges if nothing else." His eyes flicked to Ike. "You okay?"

She nodded, going shaky when she heard police-band transmissions out in the other room. "I'm fine."

But she didn't feel fine. She felt weak and wobbly and horribly turned on by the awful beauty of the violence she'd just witnessed. She didn't know if the men were dead, didn't want to know as she crossed the room, gave William a wide berth and stopped near Max, not because she was afraid of William but because she was afraid of her own response, wary of the knowledge that if he crooked a finger, she'd launch herself at him, not caring who might see.

She was acutely aware of him standing behind her, fighting to marshal his breathing and his rage. To give him time, she asked Max, "Did you and William here plan this?"

The question brought a faint burn of Ike's usual self with its corollary: *And if so, why the hell didn't you tell me about it?*

But Max shook his head and flicked a glance at his partner. "No plan. I just know the two of you too well. I knew William was going to try to head out alone tonight and I knew the moment you turned down my dinner invite, that you had every intention of going with him." He lifted one shoulder. "Since Raine is tucked in safe at the BoGen secure apartment for the time being, I figured I'd tag along in case something broke."

"Thanks," Ike said simply.

Max nodded. "That's what friends are for."

Behind her, she was conscious of movement and a deep sigh and sensed William pulling himself back together. He straightened and moved to stand beside her, touching her hand briefly as if in thanks or maybe to reassure himself that she was there and whole.

Whatever its purpose, the brief touch nearly sent her up in flames. Desire burned in her blood, and her pulse quickened, nearly drowning out Max's voice when he said, "We got Firenzetti."

That got her attention. *"What?"*

"Firenzetti," Max repeated. "We got him. He was out on the street in a limo. His driver tried to get them out by running over a cop." His lips twitched. "Let's just say the boys in blue were very thorough when they took Dominic and his driver into custody."

"You're sure of the ID?" Ike pressed, caught between surprise and relief.

"Positive. What's more, it looks like you were right about him being both the boss and your stalker. The limo contained close to a hundred pictures of you, a receipt from a flower shop, schematics of the Markham Institute and a few odds and ends that suggest he intended to bomb the press conference tomorrow, probably on the theory that if he couldn't get at the information inside Kupfer's head, he'd prevent it from being released."

"God." Sick nausea crawled in Ike's belly at the idea of a bombing and the knowledge that he'd photographed her, become obsessed with her. Why? It didn't make any sense. She was a nobody. A misfit.

"I want to see him," William grated.

Ike nodded. "Me, too."

Max looked at them both for a long minute before nodding. "I'll see what I can do."

The three of them walked out into the larger garage area, which was now brightly lit and showed signs of the vicious skirmish between the cops and Firenzetti's men. Max conferred with a tall redhead wearing street clothes. She glanced over at Ike and William, said something to Max and nodded.

He gestured for them to follow him out. "You can have five minutes, but he stays in the cruiser. Detective Blanchard isn't sure whether to believe me about The Nine, but she's not taking any chances until the feds get here."

That stopped William in his tracks. "Who'd she call?"

"I couldn't talk her out of it," Max said, obliquely confirming Grosskill's involvement. "The minute I said 'organized crime,' she was on the phone." He lifted a shoulder. "Cage's influence should buy us a few days to organize our arguments and take them higher up, at the very least."

"Right." William nodded but seemed unconvinced as they neared a cruiser parked curbside, just down the street from where they'd parked the rental a couple of hours earlier.

It seemed like days, Ike realized. So much had happened. So much had changed.

The cop in the front seat of the cruiser buzzed down the back window, saying, "You've been Mirandized, Mr. Firenzetti, so anything you say can and will be used."

The man in the backseat was familiar from the pictures Ike had managed to pull up from the databases, yet he wasn't familiar at all, she realized. His regular features, which had looked darkly handsome on film, seemed sharper and more calculating in the flesh, as did his dark, heavy-browed eyes, which went immediately to her.

His lips curved. "So lovely to meet you at last."

She instinctively took a step back, nearer William. "Same goes, under the circumstances."

He shrugged. "My arrest is merely a temporary inconvenience. I'll be out soon, and then we can be together."

She nearly shivered at the confirmation that he'd sent the notes. A shimmer of fear twisted through her and, alongside that, confusion. "Why me?"

Instead of answering, he turned to William. "Don't even begin to think this is over, Caine."

William grinned, an expression that held no humor. "Big talk." He snaked out an arm and hauled Ike to his side. "Even if you get Grosskill to spring you, she'll still be mine and not yours."

Ike knew it was all for show, that William was trying to get the bastard to admit Grosskill's involvement, that he was trying to make Firenzetti mad enough to make a mistake. But her body didn't seem to care about the distinction. Her blood buzzed at his touch and the half embrace, and her core grew heavy and warm, surging with the pound of her blood.

"So you think," Firenzetti said enigmatically and turned away, gesturing for the driver to raise the window. "I'm done talking until my lawyer gets here."

"One last question," Ike said. "What was Smith's part in all this?"

"Money," Firenzetti said despite his claim that he wasn't talking anymore. "He was nothing more than an investor and was disposed of when the time was right."

With that, he leaned back and shut his eyes, looking far too casual for a man whose entire support structure had come crashing down around him.

"Smug bastard," William muttered, but Ike detected a thread of worry behind the words. Or maybe she was projecting her own worry, her own suspicion that Firenzetti seemed far too relaxed, that he knew something they didn't.

But then William turned and looked down at her, and the vague disquiet morphed into something else entirely, something far hotter and more dangerous, akin to the desire that blazed in his eyes as he tugged her past the other cops toward their rented car. "Get in. Max will take care of the cops."

Under any other circumstances, Ike might have protested, might have demanded an explanation or fought to make the choice for herself. But what choice was left to make? Their future, at least for the next few hours, seemed immutable. The certainty had been forged in the heat that had grown as she'd watched him fight for her, reaching into something he feared rather than lose her.

More importantly, he hadn't been fighting for Eleanor. He'd been fighting for her, for Ike. For the woman she wanted to be. So she nodded and climbed into the car, letting him shut her door in a gesture of masculine possessiveness that somehow seemed just right.

There was no discussion as they sped back to the hotel. No words were necessary until they reached their floor, at the point where one door led to his room, one to hers. There, he paused and turned to her, the darkness in his eyes deepening even further by desire. "Stay with me."

"Yes," she said and put her hand in his.

Chapter Ten

He opened the door and she followed him
through, and before he could get the panel
shut and locked, she launched herself at
him, locking her legs around his waist and
hiking herself up so they were face-to-face
as his hands came up to catch her thighs,
then slide around to cup her buttocks in a
fiery caress.

But instead of diving into a kiss as her
blood and body demanded, Ike paused,
poised just above him. She cupped his face
between her palms, feeling the faint rasp of
stubble and the pound of the pulse at his
throat.

She touched her lips to his gently,
chastely, and felt him tremble. Then she
whispered, "Thank you."

The two words came from deep within her, from a place she hadn't even known existed until she'd seen him—a man of almost painful principle and honor—choose her over himself.

He caught her wrists and held her still when she would have wrapped her arms around his neck and sunk into a kiss. Eyes dark and searching, he said, "You don't need to repay me. Not like this."

Under any other circumstance, with any other man, she would've been insulted. But she knew him too well for that, knew him well enough to see through to the vulnerability beneath. So she touched her lips to his, lingering while the heat built. Then she pulled away and said, "This isn't about payment, it's about what I want. What I've wanted for a while now and was too stubborn to admit." Or maybe too scared of the consequences, she acknowledged inwardly. But those consequences seemed far away as she leaned down and kissed him again. This time she let her lips soften, let her tongue touch his.

And all restraint was lost.

William growled deep in his throat and opened to her kiss, demanding more, giving more as he spun them and pressed her lightly against the wall, using it as leverage to free his hands.

The sensations rocketing through Ike were too intense to bear, too important to escape. She angled her throat, opening herself to his touch, to his kiss, as she pulled at his soft T-shirt, seeking the tight flesh beneath.

"Ike," he said, and she gloried at the sound of her name on his lips, the promise that he knew exactly who he was kissing this time.

The fight had cleared her head and gotten her juices flowing, but that was nothing compared to the heat that screamed through her as William locked his lips on her throat, kissing his way down with a scrape of teeth and stubble while he slid his hands up her torso, then paused, teasing her. Tantalizing her.

She growled protest at the torment, then retaliated by pressing herself against the hard bulge in his jeans. He groaned and ground against her, bringing his lips back to hers in a drugging, all-encompassing kiss.

She slid her hands beneath his T-shirt so her fingers could play over his sculpted abs and the faint roughening of hair. Then she kissed him and pressed her body against his as he spun again and staggered toward the wide bed, where they collapsed in a tangle of arms and legs and half-undone clothing.

"Door locked?" she asked when his lips next left hers, only to arch against him and groan when he mumbled in the affirmative, nudged aside her biker jacket and fastened his mouth on one of her breasts, wetting the fabric with his tongue and suckling through the faintly abrasive material.

She fisted her hands in his hair, toed off her boots and hung on for the ride.

Sensations layered one atop the other as he laved her with greedy nips and long, sensuous strokes of his tongue. Ike moaned and let her head fall back. Then he was on his feet again, pulling her up with him so he could push the jacket off her shoulders and lift her shirt over her head, baring her in the fully lit room.

He stood for a moment, staring at her until she was tempted to blush, tempted to cover her breasts, which could be described as perky at best, boyish at worst. But covering up was for wimps, so instead she braced her hands on her hips and stared him down. "Well?"

"Now you're fishing." He stepped into her, and she shivered when the material of his jeans and untucked T-shirt rubbed against her bare skin. He lifted his hands until they framed her breasts, his fingers gently tracing her ribs and then working inward until she arched against him and gasped, letting her eyelids drift shut as she absorbed the pleasure. He touched his lips to hers and murmured, "Perfect. They're perfect. You're perfect."

That was so wrong it would've been funny under any other circumstance, but she was beyond laughter, beyond speech as she leaned into his touch, opening herself to him, letting him in.

Wanting to pleasure him as he was pleasuring her, she ran her hands beneath his shirt again, over the broad, bunching muscles of his back and shoulders and up to linger at the puckered bullet scars. She had the mad fleeting impulse to kiss them away. Instead she curved her fingers and raked her nails down his back, scratching lightly and loving it when he arched his spine, pressing against her touch.

She drew away from his kiss, and he anticipated her, stepping back to pull his shirt off. When he reached for her, she danced away. "Tit for tat, buster. You got to look. Now it's my turn."

He held his ground, the fire in his eyes kindling hotter when she circled around him, trailing a fingertip over his skin. "Nice."

It was better than nice, but she figured that sounded far more coherent than *holy wow,* which had been her first thought. The man was built. Based on the ripped leanness she'd felt when they'd kissed and she'd run her hands over his body, she'd expected to be impressed.

She hadn't expected perfection, but that was what stood in front of her. His wide shoulders and broad chest tied into his narrow waist in a vee of muscle and fine hair, everything angling downward, drawing her attention to the faint dip where muscles met and fused at his waistband, above the place where his arousal strained against the fly of his jeans, promising better yet to come.

A faint scar ran along his side just below his ribs, and when she moved around behind him, she saw the three bullet marks clustered high on his right shoulder, two very near each other and one lower down and likely to have caused more damage when it hit.

He wasn't perfect the way a male model or a statue could be perfect, but he was perfect for her.

Without thinking, she stood up on her tiptoes, slid her arms around his waist and touched her lips to the scars. He shuddered and reached up to press his hands on top of hers where they rested just above his zipper. She expected him to guide her downward, to where his hard flesh waited for her touch. Instead he laced his fingers through hers and squeezed.

They stood there for a long moment, standing spooned together, locked in an embrace that suddenly felt far too intimate. Far too important.

A confusing mix of emotions slapped through Ike, nearly staggering her with their intensity. There was unexpected pleasure at the moment of connection, the sensation of being in tune with another human being. But beneath that lurked an expanding kernel of fear, a little voice that had started whispering days ago and was now approaching a shout.

Pull back, it said. *Pull back now before you're in too deep and you get hurt. Think rationally. He's a good guy, a good man. When's the last time you made it work with any guy, never mind a good one?*

The answer, she knew, was never. Not one of her relationships had lasted more than a few months before her partner inevitably admitted she was too different, too out of step. Once or twice early on she'd offered to make some changes, begged them to give her another chance, but they hadn't been interested in trying.

She was too much work, they'd said. She didn't need them enough.

So they'd walked, just as William would eventually—maybe right after the case concluded, maybe a few weeks or a month later, but he'd walk. She knew that as surely as she knew she couldn't stop now, couldn't deny the heat that raged between them, the heat that had brought them together despite their differences.

She couldn't stop them from becoming lovers tonight, she knew. But she could—and would—stop it from becoming important. She could make it be about sex rather than the illusion of love.

So she slid her hands lower, carrying his along for the ride as she worked the button of his jeans and lowered the zipper, allowing his proud erection to spring free, encased only in soft cotton boxers.

Still clasping his fingers between hers, she eased his jeans and boxers down over his hips, leaving them snagged on his powerful thighs, simultaneously baring him to her touch and shackling him at her mercy.

The idea of big, bad-assed William Caine at anyone's mercy was laughable, but as she pressed herself against his back and stroked his long length with their joined hands, she felt him shudder, heard the low groan that vibrated in his chest and felt powerful.

She stroked again, curving their joined fingers around his thick rod and starting at the base, where the skin was rougher, then sliding up and out, feeling the veins and ridges and the place where his skin went soft as silk. He groaned again, a harsh, rattling sound that broke to a hiss of breath when she rubbed her thumb across the bulbous tip, collecting and spreading a drop of moisture that called to the hot, wet juices flowing within her.

He said something then—her name, maybe, or a prayer—and thrust against their joined hands, rhythmically, shuddering as his flesh grew harder and jerked with the rhythm of his heartbeat.

Ike felt that same rhythm inside her, pulsing as her hips moved to match his from behind, as he gave himself over to her, letting her lead, letting her control the rhythm while his breath rattled in his lungs and came faster, harder, matching the rhythm of their joined hands.

He pressed on her fingers, showing her how he liked it, suggesting rather than commanding. The knowledge that they were both touching him at once was brutally erotic, and Ike felt pressure building in her lungs, in her core, as the primal rhythm increased. They strained together, and then his breathing stilled, his body stilled, his whole being went rigid and he gripped their joined fingers at the base of his shaft, where the deep, pulsing explosion began.

He came on a shuddering, heaving gasp that trailed to a groan of pleasure vibrating through his entire body. His muscles locked, holding him motionless except for the flesh beneath their fingers, which pulsed rhythmically, in tune with the almost painful tugs deep within Ike.

Part of her ached for him to be inside her right now, but as the pulses slowed and his body relaxed a fraction against hers, another part—the saner part—was glad it had happened this way, that they'd had raw, down and dirty hand-job sex rather than something that ran the risk of feeling like more than it was.

As if he'd read her mind, William sucked in a breath and expelled it on a shuddering chuckle. "I'll admit, I hadn't pictured things unfolding quite like that." His back pressed into her front as he let out a long, cleansing exhalation. Then he glanced back over his shoulder. "Not that I'm complaining, mind you. But I'd like to put things back on track."

A chill spun through Ike, a dash of reality in an unreal situation. She straightened, unlinking her fingers from his. When he turned towards her, she said, "Of course. I should—"

He framed her face between his hands and kissed her. His palms were warm, his lips hot and demanding, melting the ice in an instant and bringing her blood to a boil.

When he ended the kiss and looked down at her, his expression clouded for a moment, then cleared with comprehension, though a hint of sadness remained behind. "You thought I was talking about the case." He kissed her again, taking her under with nothing more than his lips and his tongue and his gentle touch. "I wish you trusted me more than that."

Shame washed through her, along with the knee-jerk slap of irritation that she used as self-preservation. "I—"

He silenced her with a searching kiss that turned her insides to liquid heat. When she sagged against him, he said, "Do you really want to fight right now? I don't. I'd rather we try something new together."

"As long as it involves both of us getting naked," Ike said, clinging to the hope that she could keep this about sex and not something more complicated, something neither of them was ready for.

He grinned against her mouth. "Now we're on the same page."

He stepped out of his shoes, jeans and boxers, unbuttoned her pants and slid a testing, toying hand inside. He paused when he found her bare beneath.

Ike smiled as her blood drummed hard in her ears and heat pooled beneath his fingertips. "Surprise. Another of my idio-syncrasies."

"Panties make you claustrophobic?"

It was more that going commando had been yet another way to feel different and dangerous. Acting out sexually had been a way to play for her parents' attention after Donny's death. She'd thought they'd have to pry themselves out of their grief to deal with her if she made enough noise, if she acted tough enough, slept around enough, got in enough trouble.

In the end, all she'd gotten was a slutty reputation and twice-a-week counseling from a school employee with a bad comb-over.

"Let's just say that Eleanor wears panties," she murmured against his mouth. "Cotton ones with bunnies and hearts on them."

Okay, that was a bit of an exaggeration, but she needed to be sure he knew the dif-ference, that he knew he was having sex with her, Ike, not Eleanor or some sort of hybrid between the two women.

"Nothing wrong with bunnies and hearts,"

he said. Then he slid her pants down in a smooth move he'd probably practiced since early teenhood. "But I'm liking the commando thing. Makes it easier to do this."

Before she could anticipate, he dropped to his knees in front of her and looped one of her legs over his bullet-scarred shoulder, bracing her, baring her.

A hot, hard surge of lust gripped Ike when she understood his intent and she threaded her fingers through his hair, part caress, part holding on for dear life as he kissed a path up her inner thigh and her insides went to water.

Her weight-bearing leg buckled and she nearly collapsed, saving herself by grabbing onto his shoulders, then moaning when he looped an arm around her hips, anchoring her, drawing her closer as he traced his tongue inward, parting her folds with an exquisite tenderness that made her want to weep with the sensation, scream with it. Instead she dug her fingers into his hard, muscular shoulders and parted her legs wider, inviting him to do more, to do whatever he wanted.

She could count on one hand the men she'd allowed to go down on her in the most intimate of kisses, and always before she'd hung onto some thread of herself, some essence of control. Except this time, with this man. As William bent to her, loving her with his tongue and mouth, bringing her spiraling closer and closer to the edge, she realized she was in danger of having nothing held in reserve, nothing left to protect herself with.

Then it was too late, as his mouth and plundering hands found their rhythm, driving her up higher and higher still, until the pleasure vised her lungs and she was locked within the tingling, burning mix of sensation and almost painful longing that presaged orgasm. It came at her in a rush, stealing her breath and contracting her being until there was nothing but the tingling heat, and the man kneeling before her, worshiping her with his mouth.

Where before her orgasms had been hard, hot bursts she rode for all they were worth, this one slipped in almost unnoticed, pulsing and lifting her onto another level of feeling as it built and built, ever-expanding waves of pleasure that burst inside, growing in intensity until she wanted to weep.

Since that would be giving in to the pleasure, giving it more power than she was willing, she kept the tears at bay by pressing her eyelids tightly together. But she didn't stop the cries, the moans and gasps, the sound of his name on her lips. *William.*

She sagged against him as the waves lessened, remaining as pulsating aftershocks. He slid her leg from his shoulder to his waist and stood, hitching her other leg up so she could lock her ankles together above his taut buttocks, her hands still on his shoulders. With her wrapped around him, he strode to the bed. He lowered her gently and followed her down, and she heard the crinkle of plastic and the snap of latex, though she couldn't have said when he'd palmed the condom or from where.

Then he aligned their bodies, and the tip of his hard, thick shaft nudged at her entrance, teasing her, pleasuring her.

Ike's head spun, but she was aware of his body over hers, his arms braced on either side, caging her. Trapping her. She stiffened and started to voice a protest, to reverse their positions so she could bend over him and set the rhythm, control the situation.

Before she could form the words, he leaned down, touched his lips to hers and slid home.

She felt him stretch and fill her, felt the harmless hitch of pain that reminded her how long she'd been celibate—months. And how long it'd been since she'd done this with a man as large as he—years, maybe never.

Her unvoiced protest died on her lips as he withdrew and thrust again, bringing to life sensations she'd thought had been burned out by the orgasm he'd given her minutes earlier. But though she should've been sated and relaxed, her inner muscles grabbed onto him, stroking his length as he lowered his body so they were chest to chest, freeing his hands to grip her buttocks while he angled deeper, touching off sparks inside her.

"William, I... *Oh!*" Her words dissolved to a gasp as he rocked within her and a second orgasm began to build, clenching her with its utter, unassailable importance, with the feeling that what was happening to her was the single most vital thing in that moment. Her consciousness sucked inward, concentrating itself at the place where he bucked against her. His muscles bunched beneath her fingertips as he surged within her, deeper and deeper, until she felt as though he'd reached inside and grabbed a piece of her heart.

Panic jolted at the thought, but that hot rush was lost when her orgasm slammed through her unexpectedly, hard and fast and so intense it was almost painful. She bowed against him and cried out, her words sharp beneath the deep, guttural roar he gave when he came.

She felt him jerk within her and fold himself around her, holding her so tightly she couldn't breathe. But breathing wasn't necessary as her inner muscles gripped him with rhythmical pulses that matched the movements of his hard shaft and their heartbeats raced in sync.

He groaned her name, turned his head to

bury his face in her neck and tightened his arms around her as the wave washed past them, leaving pleasure to echo through their bodies in long, lingering tugs.

Then those, too, faded, and Ike's head began to clear. As it did, panic built. She was trapped beneath him, unable to breathe, unable to move or escape the slap of realizing that she'd just made a very big mistake.

She'd started off having sex and wound up making love.

ONE MOMENT, WILLIAM was lying there, sprawled across Ike, his body buzzing from the best sex of his life and his mind reverberating with the realization that it'd quite possibly been about more than body heat and friction. The next, he found himself hanging onto a tornado.

"Off!" Ike erupted into motion, pushing at him while trying to squirm out from underneath and nearly kneeing him in the process. "Get off!"

"Whoa." He rolled away from her and nearly onto the floor. "Settle down. What's wrong?"

She scrambled to a crouch, then surprised the hell out of him by vaulting off the bed and plastering herself against the far wall. She crossed her arms over her body and stood there, shaking, breathing hard, eyes wild.

As he watched, she visibly gained control of herself, straightening, dropping her arms and lifting her chin so she stood there naked but no longer looking vulnerable.

William pulled himself to a sitting position and dragged a hand through his hair. He inhaled air redolent with the scent of her and said, "Okay, you want to catch me up here? What just happened?"

"I don't generally…" She paused, then continued, but he had a feeling it wasn't what she'd originally intended when she said, "I prefer to be on top. The other way makes me feel trapped."

He felt an instant surge of compassion. "Sorry, I forgot about the claustrophobia. You should've said something sooner."

But his apology didn't seem to help matters. If anything, she grew more agitated, crossing the room to gather her clothes and pull them on in short, jerky motions. Dull red stained her cheeks, though he couldn't tell if the flush was from anger or embarrassment.

Frankly he didn't understand why she'd be either. The sex had been fantastic— they'd each come twice, for chrissakes, and there had been as much tenderness as skin on skin, if not more. Which, he realized as he watched her yank her shirt over her head, was the problem.

She never said she'd felt claustrophobic, just that she'd felt trapped, which wasn't the same thing at all.

Knowing full well there wouldn't be an encore, he rose and pulled on his boxers and jeans. He left his shirt off in a conscious effort to make her feel that she was better protected that he was.

Never once in the year or so he and Ike had known each other in passing or even in the past few weeks as they'd gotten to know each other better had he ever thought of her as insecure. But as he watched her now, only one word came to mind: *scared*. The million-dollar question was whether she was scared that he'd leave or scared that he'd stay.

When she grabbed her biker jacket, shoved the .22 in her waistband and headed for the door, he moved to block her path. "Slow down, Ike. Let's talk about this."

Normally she would have shoved him aside. Now she stumbled to a halt, as though leery of touching him. "Move, William. This isn't over just because Firenzetti is in custody. We have work to do."

"No," he contradicted. "You have running to do. Question is, are you running because the sex didn't work for you and you'd rather screw and screw?" He used the crude expression deliberately, though reducing what had happened between them to that level left a nasty taste in his mouth. "Or are you running because it worked too well for you and you don't know how to handle it?"

"Or maybe this is who I am," she countered, glaring at him. "Maybe I'm practical enough to know that we've had our moment and it's time to get back to reality."

"It's three in the morning," he said

between gritted teeth. "It won't change anything if we take five minutes here." He paused and took a deep breath, then said, "What just happened between us was pretty intense."

"Don't worry about me. I'm a big girl and I can handle myself just fine in these situations." She gestured to the door. "If you don't mind?"

He did mind, but he couldn't get past the anger that'd flared at the mention of other similar situations. In one broad sweep she'd slapped an incredible experience down to the level of her revolving-door guy policy, and that just ticked him off.

So instead of arguing and opening himself up for another hit like that one, he stepped aside. "Fine. But maybe you should ask yourself how much of this is about me and how much of it is really about you being a coward."

She hissed, infuriated. "Damn you."

"Am I really the only one who's ever put two and two together and gotten four?" His anger rose to match hers. "You do your damnedest to attract attention with the way you look and act, but then you slap at anyone who gives you that attention. You pull the claustrophobia card when it's convenient, but it's not about the actual physical space with you, is it? It's about being trapped." He spread his arms wide. "I'm not trying to trap you, Ike. I'm trying to get you to see what's standing right in front of you. I'm asking you to give this a chance."

"You don't like me," she hissed. "I'm not your type."

He exhaled a sharp, frustrated breath. "Aren't we past that yet? You're not my type, true, but it turns out I'm flexible. I respect your loyalty and your guts. I like the way you keep me on my toes, keep me guessing. And, frankly, I don't care whether you wear a dress, black leather, farmer's overalls or nothing at all, I'm still going to like you." He advanced a step, making sure she was looking into his eyes when he said, "I like you. I want to give this a try."

She stared at him for a long beat, so long he thought she might say yes. Then she turned away. "I can't, I'm sorry." She headed for the door. "It's just not worth the risk."

William felt the barb dig deep and draw blood as the door closed behind her. But could he really argue? He was a broken-down agent with an aptitude for killing and a partnership in a business that was weeks away from folding. Certainly no prize. Perhaps not worth the risk. But that didn't stop the low burn of anger from kindling in his gut, a sick twist of dismay that said this was far from over.

He walked to the window and watched her pull out in the rental, turning toward the lab. He would've guessed that as her destination. God knows it was where he would have gone—and they were more alike that she cared to admit.

He stood there a long moment, watching her taillights dwindle in the darkness. Then he cursed and headed back into the hotel room for his jacket, palming his phone and jabbing Max's number on speed dial.

This mess was almost over, and once it

was, he could walk away from her without looking back. But until then, he was damn well going to watch over her whether she liked it or not.

Chapter Eleven

Ike was still fuming as she let herself into the Kupfer lab. How dare he analyze her. What, he thought just because they'd been to bed, he had the right to crawl inside her head and take up residence? Not likely.

She stepped into the lab lobby, then stopped dead in her tracks when she heard a strangled, gurgling sigh like the one Zed had given as he'd exhaled his last breath in her arms.

Panic lunged through her. Oh, God. They'd pulled the HFH protection detail following Firenzetti's arrest. What if he'd gotten out earlier than expected?

She bolted toward Kupfer's office—and nearly tripped over him where he lay sprawled just inside the door, partway beneath the desk. She dropped to her knees and saw blood. "Dr. Kupfer. *Lukas!*"

She checked him over quickly, finding a bullet wound in his gut that oozed blackish blood, along with a cut on his scalp and a large bump on his head, suggesting someone had hit him from behind, knocking him out. Other bruises and a few gashes on his fingers indicated that he'd been worked over, an impression that was reinforced by the sight of zip ties at his wrists and ankles.

Dear Lord, she thought. He'd been tortured. Had he given up the adjunct formula? Is that why his assailant had left?

She pulled out her .22, whipped out her cell phone and speed-dialed Max's number.

The line clicked live and Max said, "We're on our way." She heard road noises in the background, along with the squeal of tires.

"Drive faster," she said and tersely outlined the situation, ending with, "Who's 'we'?"

"I've got William with me. He called to say you'd taken off in the rental."

Her blood flared at the name, but she

forced herself to be a professional. "Good. I want you two up here pronto." She hung up without waiting for a response and ignored her cell when it rang back with William's name and number in the caller ID.

No doubt he wanted her out of the building. Hell, she'd love to run, but she wasn't leaving Kupfer behind.

Just then the researcher stirred and groaned, blinking fitfully against the overhead fluorescents. He turned his head and squinted at her. "Eleanor? No," he corrected himself. "Ike."

"Well, at least your memory's intact," she said briskly. "Can you move?"

He shook his head feebly. "We both know that won't work. The bastard shot me when I wouldn't give him the formula." His eyelids drifted shut, then flickered open again. "He thinks he's won anyway, that I won't be able to publish the adjunct." He clutched at her. "You'll have to do it."

"I don't know the formula," she said, pressing a hand to his wound, which had begun to bleed in earnest again. "Just hang on and we'll get you out of here."

"No," he said. "I wrote it down just in case. I hid it in Matt's blog." His breath rattled in his lungs and he slid back toward unconsciousness, possibly for the last time.

"Damn it." Ike looked from the computer to the door and back, blood humming, trying to decide what her priorities should be.

Moments later she was seated at Kupfer's computer, bringing the machine to life.

"TRY HER AGAIN," William snapped, keeping his foot jammed on the accelerator. "She'll pick up if she knows it's you."

Maybe he shouldn't blame her for ignoring his calls—he'd pushed too hard too fast earlier. His only excuse was that he'd wanted so badly to hold onto her and convince her what they had together was real. In the end, he'd scared her.

Then he'd gotten in her face, which had sent her running even faster.

Hang on, Ike, he commanded inwardly, wishing she were still wearing her earpiece. *I'll make it up to you, I promise. We can work this out.*

He just had to get them to the Markham

Institute and get Ike clear, and they could—

"Look out!" Max threw himself across the interior of the car and jerked the wheel to one side as the windshield spiderwebbed. The car flew across the road just outside the Markham Institute, swerved and smashed into the guard shack, where it came to a shuddering halt.

William's seat belt locked on impact and the air bag detonated, buffering the jolt. He cursed, fighting his air bag and the seat belt, which held him trapped. When the belt finally gave, he yanked it aside and lurched for the door, kicking the dented panel open and moving fast, knowing whoever had shot at them wasn't likely to leave it at that. "Come on," he called to Max. "Let's move!"

There was no answer from the other side of the car.

Gut clenching, William leaned back in. In the passenger side, Max hung limp against his belt, blood trickling down the side of his head. "Max!"

William bolted around to the other side

of the car. Seeing no sign of the gunman, he yanked open the door and reached in, trying to free his partner from the seat and air bag, knowing he shouldn't move the injured man but equally sure he couldn't leave him where he was.

The scrape of a footfall on pavement was his only warning. William stood and spun in time to see four of the black-on-black bodyguards standing in a row. Three held M16s, one a rocket launcher.

He didn't bother with his own weapon. He reached into the car, heaved Max's body up and out of the vehicle and over one shoulder and turned to run, knowing it was too late when he heard the *whump* of the launcher and the scream of the rocket and the world around him lit like the Fourth of July and—

Nothing.

IKE LEFT THE COMPUTER and raced for the window at the first chatter of gunfire, reaching it just in time to see Max's rental explode in a ball of orange flame and dirty black smoke. The shock wave rattled the building, and Ike's knees gave out, sending her to the floor. She clutched the edge of the window. *"William!"*

He and Max had been coming for her. Now they were gone, just like that. In a blink. Dead.

"No!" Deep belly-wrenching sobs tore through her, doubling her over with the pain of a loss still not fully comprehended, and she heard herself babbling a litany, a mantra of denial, of prayer. *"No. Dear God, no. Please, no."*

Then a new voice spoke from the office doorway. "Hush, darling. Everything's going to be fine now."

She gasped, jerked around and scrambled to her feet, still clutching her stomach, where a screaming, empty pit had opened up, threatening to suck her inward until there was nothing else left. She stood frozen for a moment, struggling to connect what she was seeing now with what had just happened.

A light-haired, vaguely familiar man stood in the doorway, wearing a pale gray suit with a light blue shirt beneath. His steel-gray tie was perfectly knotted, his elegant brown belt perfectly flat, and when he stepped over Kupfer's motionless body to come toward her, she saw that his brown shoes were a perfect match and gleamed with a perfect shine.

His eyes were the palest blue, with pinprick-small pupils that sent a jolt of fear lancing through Ike's pain as he held out a hand. "Come with me, Celeste. Let us never be parted again."

She wanted to shout, *I'm Ike, not Eleanor and* certainly *not Celeste.* But the almost fanatical lucidity in his strange eyes warned her against the denial. So she nodded, playing along, even as she heard a secondary explosion outside and her heart ripped in two. "I'm ready…Mr. Smith?"

It was a shot in the dark, a calculated risk.

He looked at her for a long moment, then suddenly smiled, a charming expression that was ruined by those god-awful eyes. "That's my girl."

He stepped forward and took one of her hands.

Ike went for her .22 with the other.

Her captor exploded into a blur of motion. Just as she touched the butt of the small gun, he grabbed her and spun her around, snatching the weapon and tossing it on the floor beneath the desk. Using the hand he held as leverage, he whipped her arm up behind her back and leaned into her.

They wound up plastered together, with his front against her back and their arms twined together, one across her belly below her breasts, the other behind her in a painful, punishing grip.

She screamed and kicked back in a move that should have driven her boot heel into his instep, but he dodged neatly and sandwiched her legs between his, immobilizing her.

Panic spurted, and she was helpless to stop the whimper that bubbled up from her soul, could do nothing but press her eyelids together and fight for air. "Please," she whispered. "I can't breathe."

He immediately eased his grip, surprising her. "I'm sorry," he said. Then he pressed his face against her neck and inhaled. "I don't want to hurt you."

"Then let me go."

"I can't." He sounded almost sorry. "I need you. I had to have you, had to get you away from the others so you'd understand."

At first she thought he meant William and Max, and fresh pain wrested a cry from deep in her gut. Then slowly, terribly, she remembered where she'd seen him before. On the ski slope, wearing gray. He'd come to her aid and tried to convince her to stay down while they'd waited for search and rescue.

He'd really been keeping her occupied while her lover had bled out into the snow. Now he kept her captive while William's body burned.

"Bastard." Her voice shook on the word, and she couldn't even bring herself to struggle. He took the opportunity, sliding his hands along her arms and forcing her other hand behind her back, his touch remaining deliberate and almost gentle, though he twisted hard enough to break bone as he overlapped her forearms.

Tears dripped down Ike's chin, and her

mouth opened in a silent rictus of grief, of disbelief. She felt a thin strip wrap around her wrists, heard the zip as he pulled the tie tight but couldn't bring herself to care as she was swamped beneath the crushing weight of grief.

Oh, God. William.

"Come along." He lifted his hands and eased something jingling down over her head. At first she thought it was a necklace, another gift.

When he pulled it tight and snapped on a leather leash, she realized it was a choke chain.

"Damn you," she said hollowly. Some of her fighting spirit rekindled as he stepped away and knelt down to bind her ankles, more loosely than her wrists, so she could walk but not run. She sucked in a miserable breath that did nothing to fill the raw, aching void inside her. "Damn you. You'll never get away with this."

He smiled and stepped very close to her, then lifted a hand to trail a finger down her cheek. "Your face is so lovely. You remind me so much of my Celeste."

"But I'm not Celeste," she said, jumping on his admission that while she might look like the other woman, he knew they weren't the same. "I'm Ike Rombout and I can't just disappear. People will be looking for me."

His look shifted to gentle pity. "What people?"

Her throat closed on her answer. Her family had been lost to her a long time ago. Her only close friend—Max—was dead. William was dead. Who did that leave to look?

"I made myself almost invisible in your precious databases," he said. "I wiped all traces of Celeste's existence, just like I'll wipe yours after I e-mail your boss on your behalf, telling him you've decided to pull up roots and head out on your own. In a few weeks, your other acquaintances will forget to ask where you've been and you'll be nothing more than a footnote on a couple of W2 forms next year." He spread his hands. "Then you'll be nothing."

A black hole of raw panic opened up within Ike at the realization that he could do exactly that. William was right. She'd spent the past two decades trying to stand out in a conformist world, trying to get the attention and the raised eyebrows that meant she mattered. And in the end she'd wound up with so few real friends she'd be easy to forget.

Her heart raced and the walls closed in on her, stealing the oxygen from her lungs. Only there weren't any walls. They were inside her.

Tears clouded her vision and spilled free, tracking down her cheeks as she wheezed dry, choking sobs.

"That's my girl," Smith said again, seeming satisfied by her response. He cocked his head at the rising wail of sirens, then glanced down at Lukas Kupfer's motionless body. "Such a shame to lose him and Firenzetti all at once. But what the world doesn't know it lost won't hurt anyone, and Firenzetti's usefulness has ended. He may try to turn evidence when he realizes I'm not coming for him, but by then we'll be long gone." He kissed her cheek.

Ike didn't respond; she was too busy

trying not to pass out. In the end she'd failed Kupfer just as she'd failed William and Max and Zed. She'd failed thousands of kids like Jeremy, too, because she hadn't been able to find the adjunct recipe. Hell, she hadn't even been able to find Matthew's blog. She'd assumed the scientist had maintained a Web log in his son's honor, updating it with the progress of the work, but there was no evidence of such a thing on the computer. Hell, from the looks of it, he'd used the word processing package, e-mail and not much else. It seemed odd that he'd—

Her head snapped up as she realized he hadn't said *blog* at all. He'd said *dog*. Matthew's dog.

She tried to dampen the reaction, but it was already too late. Smith followed her attention to the plush toy on Kupfer's desk, and his strange pinprick eyes grew thoughtful. "What's this?"

He crossed the room, yanking her along behind by the leash, and grabbed the small stuffed animal. He felt the thing for a moment before using both hands to give it a violent twist, ripping the toy in half. Then he gave a low cry of triumph and withdrew a small stenographer's pad.

He flipped a few pages and then beamed at her with approval. "Lovely job." Hearing the sirens shut off as the cops reached the burned-out car, he said, "Time to go. The limo's waiting for us on the other side of the building."

He dragged her out the door, not pausing when she tripped on Kupfer's still-warm body and fell to her knees. She gagged against the choke chain and struggled to get up with her hands bound behind her, knowing from the implacable set of his shoulders and the blank unconcern in his eyes that he'd choke her to death rather than let her slow him down.

Part of her was tempted to let herself fall, but she was too damn stubborn for that, so she gritted her teeth and struggled onward, staring at Smith's back while the hatred grew.

Chapter Twelve

To Ike's surprise, they were only in the limo for twenty minutes or so before the driver pulled into a long tree-lined driveway and stopped in front of a stately old mansion that looked like a restored Colonial on steroids.

"It's a rental," Smith said, his expression shifting to one that sent her skin crawling. "I set it up in case Kupfer needed additional persuasion to share his recipe. That didn't go exactly as planned, but no matter." He touched the breast pocket of his gray suit, where he'd tucked the small notebook. "I have the formula and I have you. We'll stop here long enough for me to make other arrangements and to let you freshen up. I'm sure you'd like to change out of those ridiculous clothes."

Ike bowed her head, hoping she looked utterly broken. It wasn't far from the truth. Her whole body ached with the pain of loss, with the knowledge that, like the terrible things she'd said the last time she'd visited Donny in the hospital, the last words she'd hurled at William had been angry, unkind ones. And, she admitted privately, she'd been wrong. So much of what she'd done, so many of the choices she'd made had been to protect herself from being hurt.

She'd thought being a rebel meant she was brave. In reality, she'd been a coward, hiding behind her look and attitude.

When the driver opened the limo door, Smith unhooked her leash from where he'd tied it to the door handle as an added precaution. "Come." Using the slip chain as leverage, he dragged her up and out of the vehicle and led her to the front door. When her feet tangled in the zip ties and she stumbled, he yanked on the leash until she gagged. "Watch your step. We wouldn't want you to hurt yourself."

He led her into the house, where age

competed with modern upgrades at every turn. Her childhood in an old Vermont home and many weekends spent antiquing with her parents told her the bones of the structure probably dated from the Revolutionary War. Somewhere along the line, though, maybe more than once, the place had been gutted and redone, leaving a central staircase to spiral from the front entrance, upward through three levels of rooms ringing a central open space that no Colonial architect would have conceived.

The walls were covered in damask fabric above polished maple wainscoting, the rugs were new-looking Orientals and the furniture was expensive modern Scandinavian. The whole effect was jarring and somehow cheap, despite the obvious upgrades.

Ike surreptitiously counted heads as Smith dragged her up the spiraling staircase—the driver followed them in and headed for the kitchen, where she saw two other black-on-black bodyguards seated at a table. She glimpsed two other men hunched over computers in a room on the second floor, bringing the total to five bodyguards plus her captor, though there could easily be others she hadn't seen.

"In here." Smith spun the dial on a heavy-duty padlock bolted into the door frame of a room off the stairwell. He popped the lock, opened the door and pushed her through. "My apologies on the decor. This room was intended for Kupfer, but it's also the only secure space in the house. You'll be safe here."

Safe from what? she wanted to ask, but then she got a good look around and the question died in her throat.

The opulent suite was done in polished wood and brass, with soft fabric accents in pale, feminine colors. The main room was large and high-ceilinged, holding a collection of deeply cushioned sofas and chairs, along with a plasma TV and a top-of-the-line entertainment center. In one corner, a small refrigerator was set beneath a bar, with a pair of fixed stools tucked nearby, creating an eating nook. Two doors led off the main space, both open, one leading to a bedroom done in the same pastel color scheme, the other leading to a bathroom with a sunken tub and pale marble on the floor and walls.

In the center of the seating area, a plastic tarp had been thrown over the rug. In the middle of it sat a heavy metal chair that had shackles welded to the armrests and legs, and heavy nylon belts at the waist and neck. Nearby, a tray of wickedly pointed instruments rested atop an elegantly carved mahogany side table, along with an assortment of vials and syringes, all pristine and waiting for a patient.

Ike suppressed a shudder, but Smith saw her reaction, and his lips tipped up at the corners. "I see that we understand each other. Good. I'll leave you alone to freshen up, but first I need to take care of one important detail."

He tugged her into the center of the room and scooped a sharp knife from the tray.

Fear shot through Ike. She shrieked and stumbled back, but he yanked on the choke chain to bring her to heel. The ankle ties snagged her feet and she went down in a heap, crying out when he knelt across her belly, pinning her. Then he used the knife methodically, not to stab her but to strip her.

He cut away her tight black pants and cursed to find her bare beneath. Surprising her, he tossed the ragged remains of her pants across her midsection before he turned his attention to her upper half, hacking at her favorite jacket until the tough leather yielded beneath his blade, then cutting through her T-shirt, the one William had taken off her the day before.

Tears stung her eyes at the memory, at the humiliation of being stripped by her enemy.

Just cut me, she wanted to say. *Or, better yet, let me go and* fight *me, you coward.*

But he did neither of those things, gathering her shredded clothes and removing her boots with a disturbingly gentle touch. He pulled off the choke chain, stood and gathered the rest of the knives, along with the syringes and drugs. Then he turned for the door, which had remained open throughout the process.

Ike saw four of the bodyguards gathered

in the hallway outside her room and cringed at their blatant stares.

"You all have work to do," Smith snapped, dispersing his men. Then he turned back to her and said, "I had some of Celeste's clothes moved in here for you. I'm sure you'll be more comfortable once you're suitably attired. I have some things to take care of." He patted his breast pocket. "We'll leave in an hour. Be ready."

His strange pinprick eyes held the oddest expression, seeming stuck between love and hate as he shut the door. Moments later, Ike heard the heavy padlock click into place, sealing her in.

She wanted to jump up, pound on the door and scream, *Why me?* What had she done to attract him, to make him want her, to make him hate her?

Fear and frustration welled up, suffusing her, threatening to drown her. Who was she to think she could go up against someone like Smith, who'd somehow led The Nine without making a mark on the information superhighway?

Surprisingly that small, sarcastic voice

inside her, the one that usually shot her down, piped up to say, *You're Ike. Never forget it.*

"That's right," she said aloud, drawing a bit of empty bravado from the words. "I'm Ike Rombout and I'm not going to let you get away with this. I'm going to take you down or die trying."

Now she just had to figure out how.

IT TOOK IKE A SOLID ten minutes to get herself out of the zip ties by abrading them against a sharp corner she pried away from the refrigerator housing. Once she was free, she headed for the bedroom and found three flowery sundresses in the closet, though no shoes or underthings.

It's better than being naked, she thought as she pulled on a ruffled pale pink number that grabbed her at the waist and nearly touched the floor. *But not by much.*

Then she paused. Behind the dresses, a framed eight-by-ten photograph sat on an empty shoe rack at the back of the closet. It showed a lovely woman wearing a long flowered dress a decade out of date. Her honey-colored hair was waist length and flowed down her back, and her features were sharply exotic and expertly made up.

For Ike, it was like looking in a distorted mirror—one that showed things not as they really were but as they might have been. The picture didn't look like the woman she'd been before this all began, didn't look like her made-over disguise of Eleanor. It looked like a blend of the two.

And, she realized as a ball of ice congealed in her stomach, the woman in the photo looked very much like she did at that moment.

Her skin crawled at the touch of the clingy fabric, at the realization that the dress had belonged to a dead woman. She had to assume Celeste was dead, either by accident or murder, because she couldn't imagine Smith letting her go free.

And just as Ike knew he would have killed Celeste rather than allowing her to leave him, she knew he wouldn't let her go free either.

"We'll see about that," she said aloud. But she knew escape wouldn't be easy. He might pretend he'd intended this room for Kupfer's torture, but he'd also brought Celeste's clothes and picture to the rented mansion, which suggested he'd planned to bring her back here all along.

He'd killed Zed to get to her, Ike thought, her eyes filming. He'd killed William. One had been her lover, one had been her love, though she was just now realizing it, a few hours too late.

Grief rose up and swamped her, weakening her resolve and turning her legs to water. She sank down just outside the closet, pulling her knees to her chest and pressing her face atop them. She hugged her legs and rocked, keening for lost people, lost chances. Her tears soaked into the light fabric of a dead woman's dress and weakness rose up and claimed her. *I can't do this,* she thought miserably. *I can't.*

Worse, she wasn't sure she wanted to. Wouldn't it be easier to just give up?

Come on, a voice said inside her head. *We both know giving up isn't your style.*

Her head came up and her heart lodged in her throat. That hadn't sounded like her voice. It'd sounded like William's voice transmitted through the small earpiece.

She touched her ear on a brief spurt of hope, then let her hand fall away, knowing the transmitter wasn't there. William wasn't there. Except in a way, he *was* there, sitting on her shoulder as he'd been when she first went undercover. *Get up,* she imagined him saying. *He's erasing you from existence as we speak. In less than an hour he'll be on the move, and then God only knows what he'll do with you, where he'll take you.* A pause and then, *Are you going to let him get away with this? Are you going to let him license the adjunct and use the money to rebuild The Nine?*

A small spurt of anger drove Ike to her feet.

"No, damn it," she said aloud, taking strength from hearing the words. "I'm going to stop him." For Zed. For Kupfer. For Jeremy and all the other patients who'd been hurt by The Nine over the years.

And most of all for William.

Blood beginning to burn, she left the bedroom, looking for a weapon—something, anything she could use to attack when the door next opened. As she searched, she was struck once again by the almost haphazard way modern design had been slapped atop an antique structure.

It was a huge old house, she thought as she moved through the main room, skirting the big metal chair. And large houses had servants' stairs and dumbwaiters, right? In addition, houses built during the Revolution often had hidden spaces for concealing smuggled goods or deserting soldiers. She knew because she'd grown up in just such a house.

"There's no guarantee," she told herself, but that didn't stop her from making a circuit of the room, tapping the outer walls at regular intervals but hearing nothing unusual.

Then she moved into the bathroom—and struck pay dirt. A section of wallpapered drywall opposite the sunken tub echoed hollowly compared to the surrounding surfaces.

"Bingo," she said, adrenaline spurting. Without another thought, she grabbed the heavy porcelain top off the toilet and swung it at the wall.

The blow punched through with a hollow, echoing sound that was followed by a rattling as chunks fell inward and down what looked like a vertical chimney lined with thin slats of old, rough-hewn wood fastened with pegs and rose-head nails. Probably a dumbwaiter shaft without the dumbwaiter, she figured. Perfect.

"Damn, I'm good," she said, some of her normal cockiness returning as she hit the wall a few more times, clearing most of the rectangular opening.

Then she stuck her head through and froze. The shaft was very narrow, the space beyond it very dark.

She straightened slowly and backed away as her breath tightened in her lungs. *I can't do this,* she thought. *No way.*

Except there was no *other* way, she knew. It was either the shaft or she let Smith win.

Taking a deep breath, she hiked up her skirt, climbed up on the vanity, grabbed onto either side of the opening and pulled herself through. Her stomach clenched hard as she scooted up so she could get her legs all the way in, so she was braced in the shaft with her back against the rough slats on one side, her shins and forearms pressed against the rough ladderlike surface on the other.

It was a seriously tight fit. Beads of sweat broke out on her forehead, and her arms started to tremble with the strain of holding herself.

You can do this, Ike, she told herself, trying to believe that she was just as tough, just as badass in ruffles and bare feet than she was in leather and boots. *For William.*

With his image at the forefront of her mind, she started shimmying down the shaft just as she heard the padlock rattle and the door to her room open. Moments later Smith's voice bellowed, "Where the hell is Celeste?"

Ike's already high pulse accelerated to rapid-fire, and she started wriggling down as fast as she could, knowing there was no way he wouldn't see the mess in the bathroom.

Sure enough, she heard an enraged shout moments later. "In here!"

Heavy footfalls sounded above her, echoing all around her in the musty shaft. Cobwebs coated her arms and legs, and each of her motions dislodged a shower of dirt and dust, clogging her nose and mouth and making her want to cry out.

Then, mercifully, the surface beneath her hands and knees went smooth as the shaft opened onto another panel of drywall. She'd reached the next level down.

"Shoot her!" one of the bodyguards shouted from above, but Smith countermanded the command.

"No shooting," he ordered, his words clipped and coldly furious. "Two of you watch the bottom floors. You—get in there and bring her out." Ike risked a look up to where Smith was silhouetted against the light from the bathroom. She could see nothing of his shadowed features, but his eyes gleamed with pinprick hatred that was reflected in his voice when he said, "Once again I offer you everything and you spit in my face, Celeste. And once again you'll have to pay the price for your rebellion."

Her fury overruled her good sense, and she shouted, "My name is Ike!" She heaved, pushing as hard as she could with her legs and arms, pressing her back against the rough boards harder and harder until her muscles shook with the effort.

Then, mercifully, the drywall cracked, then broke, ripping through the wall covering. She shoved again, then kicked her way through one floor down, aware of Smith's shouts and the thunder of booted feet.

Then she was free. She spilled out in another bathroom, this one done in blue and yellow. Scrambling to her feet, she headed for the main room of a suite very much like the one upstairs, only without the eating nook. She yanked open the door and hit the hallway running.

Her original plan had been to sneak into the computer room and try to contact Zach Cage. Now her only hope was to get outside on to the main road. The houses in the area had seemed few and far between, but if she could flag down a car and—

"There she is!" a male voice shouted.

Ike didn't look back. She ran, flying down the hallway barefoot, then skidding down the stairs two at a time and—

A heavy weight hit her from behind, driving her forward and down. She landed face-first with one of the bodyguards on top of her.

"Got her!" The bodyguard dragged her up, holding fast as she writhed and bucked against him. "What do you want me to do with her?"

"Hold her," Smith said. "I'll be right there."

The bodyguard spun her to face the leader of The Nine, who approached and held out a hand. One of the other bodyguards slapped a Glock into his palm.

"It's a pity we don't have more time," Smith said. "I think you would've come around to my way of thinking with a little encouragement. But I find myself in the position of having to cut my losses sooner than expected." Before Ike could wonder what had changed, he lifted the Glock, racked the action and raised it to point the muzzle at her forehead. "Goodbye again, Celeste."

Helpless to escape, Ike braced herself for the roar of gunfire. Instead the front door exploded inward and a figure stood in the opening for a brief second, haloed by the daylight, seeming for a moment more avenging angel than man. Then he flung himself at Smith with a warrior's roar, and Ike knew it wasn't an angel or a ghost.

It was William.

Chapter Thirteen

For a moment Ike thought she was seeing things, that her mind had conjured up William's image in a final farewell. Then their eyes met and heat flared, hope flared, warming her and telling her it wasn't a mirage at all.

William was here. He was alive.

And he'd come for her, just in time.

Love blossomed through her, absolute and overwhelming, along with almost paralyzing relief. He'd survived the explosion. *Thank you, God,* she thought with utter clarity.

William lunged across the entryway and flung himself at Smith, who swung around, took aim and fired. Then there was little more than a blur of men and fists as William dived in and fought, pummeling the other man with brutal punches. His eyes were wild and angry, and when two of the bodyguards moved in and pulled him off, he exploded, spinning into that fluid fighting style he used with such lethal grace. Two of the bodyguards went down immediately, gurgling, and two others dropped moments later.

Smith struggled to his feet, grasping at his belly, and headed for Ike and the man who held her.

"William!" Ike screamed.

One moment he was across the room and the next minute he was there, dropping the man who held her and pulling her into a protective embrace as Smith scooped a fallen weapon from the floor and took aim.

Smith fired at the same moment William sent a stiff-fingered jab into his throat.

The bullet went wide and shattered a nearby wall sconce. Smith gurgled, his eyes rolled back in his head and he collapsed in an inglorious heap just inside the front door.

For a few seconds there was a silence so

absolute that Ike could hear her heart begin to beat once again, making her aware that it had stopped when she thought William might die.

If that wasn't love, if the huge, awful, terrifying relief she felt now wasn't love…

No, she thought on a burst of heat and excitement and giddy, silly happiness, that was most definitely love.

Outside, she heard booted feet and sporadic gunfire, suggesting that William had brought backup and lots of it. But in the house itself there was only silence, only the two of them standing nestled close together, their hearts beating in sync.

Ike looked up and found him looking down at her, eyes dark with an emotion she couldn't quite interpret.

"William?" she said, her voice tentative. Then, realizing that tentative was Eleanor's fallback position, not hers, she squared her shoulders beneath the gauzy dress and said, "Okay, here's the deal. You were right about me being a coward, but you were wrong about one thing. You were wrong when you said I was missing what was

right in front of me. You're in front of me."
While the room took a long, lazy spin
beneath her feet, she sucked in a breath
and said, "I love you."

WILLIAM CLOSED HIS eyes on a sigh and let
the words pour through him, healing the
broken places. He let the feel of her body
against his steady him, filling the hollow
spot deep within.

"I thought I was going to be too late," he
said, his voice rough with emotion, with
the despair that had dogged him as he and
his unexpected allies had raced to save her.

"Your timing was just right," she said,
touching his face. "It was perfect."

He looked down at her, farther down that
he was used to without the added height of
her heels to equalize them. But though she
was shorter than he, she had complete and
utter power over him. "Say it again," he
demanded.

He expected a sharp retort. Instead she
stood on her toes and pressed her lips to
his. "I love you."

Inside him, a great, tight knot unraveled

and everything went still. He leaned into the kiss and slipped his arms around her waist, feeling the long, lean muscles of her back beneath the soft material of an unfamiliar dress. Part Eleanor, part Ike, she was all his.

He broke the kiss and leaned his forehead against hers. "That's a relief, because I love you right back."

Her smile was pure joy, her kiss hot, sweet magic that swept him up and left him reeling until another voice broke in, saying, "Ahem. You two mind if we drag Smith out now and Mirandize him?"

William pulled away from Ike long enough to glare and say, "You're interrupting, Grosskill."

That got Ike's attention. She shifted position so her body was almost entirely in front of his and gave the sharp-faced man in the doorway an up-and-down inspection.

"Grosskill, huh?" Her tone made it clear she was less than impressed by the Bureau man, who had a large red patch on his jaw that would soon go purple with bruising.

William had been grateful for the agents who'd gotten him and Max out of the way just before the car went up in flames and he'd been grateful for their help in subduing the men outside the Markham Institute and rushing Max and Kupfer to a nearby hospital.

He'd been far less happy to learn of Grosskill's covert op, another one of his "left hand doesn't know what the right hand is doing" plans that could've gotten everyone killed.

Ike looked up at William. "What's he doing here?" She indicated Grosskill with a jerk of her head.

Fairness compelled William to say, "He got Max and me out of the car just before it went up." He paused. "It turns out I did see him in the hall that day. The order to lay off The Nine came from very high up, but Michael here didn't like the smell of it, so he cleared the fourth floor and set up surveillance while pretending to the bureau that he was working on something else. Guess he's grown into some instincts in his old age."

"Gee, thanks." Grosskill scowled, but the sarcasm lacked its full edge. When William gestured for him to go on, the FBI agent said, "It took us some time to figure out who you were, Miss Rombout. That was a hell of a cover."

"Thanks. Think I'm FBI material?"

William tightened his fingers on her shoulders and aimed a don't-even-think-about-it glare at Grosskill, who side-stepped her question and continued, "We'd begun to suspect Smith and knew he was nearby, but we never expected him to move so fast, or take a hostage. That isn't his usual MO."

"I reminded him of someone named Celeste," she said. "He must've noticed the resemblance when I was working for Max on the Thriller case, when The Nine targeted Raine's drug. He…" She trailed off, then swallowed hard before continuing. "He killed Zed himself. I saw him. He was one of the skiers. If I'd just known then…"

William drew her back against his chest

and wrapped his arms around her, holding her loosely so she wouldn't feel trapped. "What's done is done. We've got him now, and he won't be hurting anyone ever again. I'll see to that."

"We all will," Grosskill said, and a light of anger kindled in his eyes. "I'm going to kick this to the top and see what happens. Ten gets you a hundred someone big is going to fall out of the government tree."

"Let us know what we can do to help," William offered. "If it's in electronic form, Ike here can find it for you."

"I'd take you both in a heartbeat," the FBI director said.

"Really?" Ike cocked her head. "What sort of benefits are we talking about?" When William growled, she laid her hands over his and squeezed, encouraging him to tighten his arms around her. "Don't worry, I'm just kidding. I think I've finally figured out what I want to be when I grow up."

"Mine?" William asked, only half joking.

"Absolutely." She slanted him a look. "I have a feeling Vasek & Caine investigations is about to get very popular. You thinking of hiring a receptionist anytime soon?"

"No," he said as everything clicked into place inside his heart. "But I think Max might be amenable to taking on a third partner."

Her smile started as pure joy, then morphed to worry, and she said in a small voice, "Then Max is…"

"He and Kupfer are both alive." He glanced over at Grosskill. "Any updates?"

"Both critical but stable," the FBI director confirmed with a small smile. "Come on, I'll give you a lift to the hospital." His eyes flicked to William. "I know you well enough to guess that's your first destination, and if half of what I've heard about Ms. Rombout is true, she'll be racing you for the door."

William pressed a kiss to her temple. "That's my girl."

The simple truth of the words set up a warm glow in his heart.

WHEN THEY REACHED Springfield Hospital, they learned that Max and Kupfer were both still in recovery from their various surgeries and it would be an hour or more before they could have visitors. Technically it was family only, but Grosskill had a quick conversation with the desk nurse and cleared it for Ike and William to get in.

"He doesn't seem like quite the monster you portrayed," Ike murmured aside to William as they watched the FBI director sweet-talk the nurse while keeping a commandeered land line phone to his ear, getting a status report on booking Smith and his thugs and processing Firenzetti.

"I think he's matured into his position," William said, looking at his former boss with thoughtful eyes. Then he glanced at her and lifted one shoulder. "Heck, maybe we've both grown up."

"I know the feeling." Ike reached for his hand, but he seemed suddenly distant. She wanted to ask if he was okay, but it seemed like a stupid question, given that they were in a hospital, both waiting on word of a good friend.

She had a feeling it was more than that and wasn't surprised when he disengaged his hand from hers. "You okay waiting here? Raine should be arriving any minute, and I'll be back by the time they let Max have visitors."

"I'm a big girl," Ike said, words faintly clipped. "I don't need a keeper."

Normally that sort of reply would've gotten a rise out of him. Now, though, he merely dropped a brief kiss on her lips. "See you in a bit, then."

He walked away, his shoulders tense beneath a light coat he'd borrowed from one of Grosskill's men. The sight of the yellow *FBI* stenciled on the navy jacket sent a shimmer of worry through Ike's midsection.

He and Grosskill had made peace. What if he was regretting what he'd said about her becoming a partner? What if he wanted to go back into the Bureau and couldn't think of a way to tell her?

Don't borrow trouble, Einstein, she reminded herself when the panic came, not because she was trapped but because she thought she felt him slipping away already. *If you love something set it free, and all that rot.*

Or, more rationally, if you love something,

fight for it tooth and nail, which was more her style.

"He's a good man," Grosskill said unexpectedly from beside her.

Ike hadn't noticed his approach, but she hid the flinch and answered simply, "Yes."

She braced herself for an explanation of why William should return to the Bureau, how his country needed him, regardless of what she needed.

Instead the FBI director leaned over the admissions desk, returned the borrowed handset and said, "Ms. Rombout is with us. Give her whatever she needs." He straightened and nodded to her. "It's been a pleasure. We'll be in touch."

He departed with those ominous words ringing in the sterile hospital air. Ike watched him go, trying to figure out what the hell had just happened and why.

"Ma'am?" the nurse said, drawing her attention. "Can I get you anything?"

"No, thanks," she said automatically, then said, "Wait, yes, actually. I need to borrow a Web-linked computer and a phone."

Then she pressed a hand to her suddenly

queasy stomach. She couldn't fight for William until he returned and they were face-to-face, but there were two other things she could do in the interim, one of which she'd put off for far too long.

IT TOOK WILLIAM THREE stores and an hour and a half to find exactly what he was looking for, and his nerves were nearly shot by the time he got back to the hospital. A couple of calls to the front desk had assured him that neither Max nor Kupfer had suffered any setbacks while he was gone. However, the same could not be said of him and Ike, he realized when he entered the waiting room and saw her sitting beside Raine.

She'd gone somewhere for a change of clothing and had replaced the ruffled dress with trim slacks, a tailored shirt and high-heeled boots. They were all black, of course, but more feminine than severe, and she'd swept the long hair away from her face with a clip of some sort, leaving a few wisps to drift down and soften the effect.

She's lovely, he thought on a fist of

emotion. Unfortunately she also looked thoroughly upset.

Oh, hell. He'd given her too much time to think about their half-assed conversation, to consider what it would mean for them to make a go of it. A relationship, maybe even marriage. The ultimate emotional trap to a woman like her.

Raine's eyes lit and her lips curved slightly when she saw him. "You made it back."

"Of course." William advanced into the room, his eyes fixed on Ike, who deliberately looked away. "I wouldn't let Max down." The words were directed at Ike. *I won't let you down. Trust me, please.*

Before either of the women could respond, the far door swung open and a nurse waved them in. "You can see your friends now."

Raine was up and through like a shot, leaving Ike and William to follow behind her. Where only a couple of hours earlier it had been easy for him to reach for her hand, now William found himself hesitating.

He'd made love to Ike. He loved her. Yet

he didn't know how to start now, what to say. This was too big, too important to screw up.

His timing had to be perfect.

Raine gave a glad cry and rushed past the nurse into a room off the long hospital hallway, arms outstretched as though she was going to fling herself onto her heavily-bandaged husband. Just at the edge of the bed, she slammed on the brakes and put both hands to her mouth, eyes brimming with worry and love. Her voice came out in a broken whisper when she said, "Max?"

"We got him." His eyes opened and fixed on her. "He's never coming after you ever again. You're safe."

To everyone's surprise, Raine cut loose with a very un-Raine-like curse and glared down at her husband. "If you think that's the most important thing right now, then you're an idiot." Her eyes filled when she said, "You could've died. You almost did. I'd rather spend the rest of my life running from The Nine than lose you." Her breath hitched, her strong facade crumbled and she burst into tears.

Max smiled and opened his arms to her. "Come here."

As husband and wife embraced, first tentatively and then with increasing force, William turned away.

Ike followed suit. "Looks like they could use a moment. Let's check on Kupfer."

When they reached the scientist's room, they found him in tougher shape than Max, but incredibly his spirits seemed excellent. He grinned when he saw them in the doorway. Or, rather, his face lit when he saw Ike, which sent a quick stab of jealousy through William.

"Lucille called," he said, reaching a hand out to Ike. "How did you know?"

"I saw the picture on your desk." She shrugged, looking faintly uncomfortable with the sentiment. "So I looked her up. She sounded nice on the phone."

With that, William's jealousy fled and was replaced with surprise. Every time he thought he had Ike figured out, she did something unexpected.

"She's wonderful." Kupfer's eyes filled. "When Matthew died, I kept working, probably worked harder than I had before. I should've been there for her, but I couldn't be, because it was my failure. I let him die."

"You did everything a man could do," Ike said quietly, not bothering with the easy platitudes. "And you'll have a chance now to keep other kids from dying. Matt would've liked that."

"Yeah, he would've." Kupfer nodded, wincing when the motion pulled on his injuries. "Lucille's flying in tonight to see me. He would've liked that, too."

"I'll keep my fingers crossed for you. And here. I think you'll be needing this." She pulled a small spiral-bound notebook from her back pocket and handed it to Kupfer. Then she squeezed his hand and turned for the door.

She pushed past William and back out into the hall, walking with her characteristic loose-limbed stride, but William was aware of another level to the motion—a deep tension, an almost frenetic sense of pace, as though she was afraid to slow down long enough for them to have the conversation they both knew was necessary.

She stopped at the doorway to Max's room, then turned away with a half smile on her lips. "I'd say they need a few more minutes. They look…busy." She paused, then said thoughtfully, "I wasn't sure at first, but they fit just right. He needs to be needed, and I think he's starting to figure out that he needs her right back. That's good." She nodded as though concluding a long-running internal conversation.

Seeing the opportunity he'd been waiting for, if not the ambience, William took a deep breath and said, "We need to talk."

He thought he saw a flash of fear in her eyes before she banked the expression and turned away from the door. "I know. I've been thinking about what you said before."

His mouth went dry with the fear that he was about to be royally brushed off. "You mean the I-love-you part. I mean it, you know."

If anything, that seemed to increase her tension. She knotted her fingers at her waist, an uncharacteristic sign of nerves. "I was talking about what Grosskill said about you returning to the FBI."

"I don't—" he began, but she crossed to him unexpectedly and laid one index finger on his lips, interrupting.

"Let me finish. I know I'm supposed to promise to follow you to the ends of the earth, but I think we both know that's Eleanor's style, not mine. I'm selfish and spoiled and I want what I want, which is for you to turn him down. I want us to live together in New York. I want us to work together. I want us to *be* together. None of that long-distance crap." She lifted her chin as though daring him to let her down. "There, I've said it."

She might've been all Ike attitude on the outside, but now that he knew her better, William could see the vulnerability beneath, the insecurity that she might've blamed on her cover story or the makeover but was truly part of her human core.

"You haven't said the magic words," he said, warmth unfurling within him as he finally started to believe that this just might work out after all.

"Pretty please?" she sassed, getting that go-to-hell glint back in her eye. Then her voice and expression softened to a woman's warmth and she said, "I love you."

Three simple words, right out there for all the world to hear.

Knowing that it was right, William reached inside his borrowed coat and pulled out a flat jeweler's box. He flipped it open and held out the offering. "Then marry me."

IKE GAPED AS STUNNED amazement collided with joy inside her. The large gemstone was matte black but glittered from deep within as invisible facets caught the overhead lights. At first she thought it was a naked stone for her to set the way she wanted. Then she realized what he'd bought to symbolize their engagement, and her eyes filled.

It was a black diamond earring.

"I figured you'd be needing a new one now that Odin and The Nine are finished." He offered the box. "So…what do you say?"

She didn't say anything, just reached out, released the earring from its velvet-lined holder and slid the post through the top hole in the rim of her right ear. The weight made her feel whole again. It made her feel like Ike again.

"Is that a yes?" he asked, his face finally betraying nerves that mirrored her own.

"Yes," she said, the word bursting out of her on an explosion of pure joy. She threw herself at him, wrapping her arms around his neck and her legs around his waist, glorying when he caught her and held her tight and not a hint of panic came. "Yes!"

His eyes darkened with passion and he whispered, "I love you, Ike Rombout."

They kissed on a burst of heat and power and joy, along with the great, spiraling relief that the danger was over, Odin was caught, Zed was avenged and they could move forward from there, into the future uncluttered by ghosts of the past.

Or almost uncluttered, Ike realized when she heard a small sound behind her, broke the kiss and turned her head to see an older couple standing in the hallway maybe twenty feet away. The man was tall and unbowed, his hair still dark, but years of sadness were etched in his face. The woman was smaller and light-haired, beautiful despite the sharp angles of her face—or maybe because of them.

Ike's heart clutched at the realization that her parents looked so much older than she remembered.

Her father took a step forward, into a faint hallway shadow that softened the lines on his face and darkened his hair, and suddenly she saw Donny in the shape of his eyes and the square line of his jaw. His voice trembled when he said, "Eleanor?"

William stiffened in shock, probably realizing that was actually her given name, one she'd legally changed long ago as yet another in a long list of defiant acts. His arms went lax, allowing her to slide down and turn to face her parents on her own feet.

"Hey, Mom, Dad, thanks for coming." It had been a surprise to find them still in the southern Vermont town where she'd grown up, though she couldn't have said why. But as far as Ike was concerned, finding them less than an hour away had been a sign that it was time—if not past time—for the three of them to reconnect. Now she took a step toward them, then reached a hand back for William, feeling that click of connection when he grabbed on. "I'd like you to meet William. He's my…" She paused, feeling as though this first use of the word was a milestone. "He's my fiancé."

"Pleased to meet you." William shot her a look that promised a hell of a conversation later and shook hands with her father first and then her mother. "Ike, er, Eleanor is a wonderful woman."

As the first moment of awkwardness eased, Ike felt laughter bubble up in her throat, a combination of excitement, relief and joy as she realized that she was pieces of both women, Ike and Eleanor. In bringing down Odin she'd found herself, and in doing so she'd found her other half, her lover and future husband

Her partner. William.

* * * * *

*Don't miss Jessica Andersen's next
Harlequin Intrigue, CLASSIFIED BABY,
the final installment of
BODYGUARDS UNLIMITED,
DENVER, COLORADO,
on sale in August 2007!*

Dante Raintree stood with his arms crossed as he watched the woman on the monitor. The image was in black and white to better show details; color distracted the brain. He focused on her hands, watching every move she made, but what struck him most was how uncommonly *still* she was. She didn't fidget or play with her chips, or look around at the other players. She peeked once at her down card, then didn't touch it again, signaling for another hit by tapping a fingernail on the table. Just because she didn't seem to be paying attention to the other players, though, didn't mean she was as unaware as she seemed.

"What's her name?" Dante asked.

"Lorna Clay," replied his chief of security, Al Rayburn.

"At first I thought she was counting, but she doesn't pay enough attention."

"She's paying attention, all right," Dante murmured. "You just don't see her doing it." A card counter had to remember every card played. Supposedly counting cards was impossible with the number of decks used by the casinos, but there were those rare individuals who could calculate the odds even with multiple decks.

"I thought that, too," said Al. "But look at this piece of tape coming up. Someone she knows comes up to her and speaks, she looks around and starts chatting, completely misses the play of the people to her left—and doesn't look around even when the deal comes back to her, just taps that finger. And damn if she didn't win. Again."

Dante watched the tape, rewound it, watched it again. Then he watched it a third time. There had to be something he was missing, because he couldn't pick out a single giveaway.

"If she's cheating," Al said with something like respect, "she's the best I've ever seen."

"What does your gut say?"

Al scratched the side of his jaw, considering. Finally, he said, "If she isn't cheating, she's the luckiest person walking. She wins. Week in, week out, she wins. Never a huge amount, but I ran the numbers and she's into us for about five grand a week. Hell, boss, on her way out of the casino she'll stop by a slot machine, feed a dollar in and walk away with at least fifty. It's never the same machine, either. I've had her watched, I've had her followed, I've even looked for the same faces in the casino every time she's in here, and I can't find a common denominator."

"Is she here now?"

"She came in about half an hour ago. She's playing blackjack, as usual."

"Bring her to my office," Dante said, making a swift decision. "Don't make a scene."

"Got it," said Al, turning on his heel and leaving the security center.

Dante left, too, going up to his office. His face was calm. Normally he would leave it to Al to deal with a cheater, but he was curious. How was she doing it? There were a lot of bad cheaters, a few good ones, and every so often one would come along who was the stuff of which legends were made: the cheater who didn't get caught, even when people were alert and the camera was on him—or, in this case, her.

It was possible to simply be lucky, as most people understood luck. Chance could turn a habitual loser into a big-time winner. Casinos, in fact, thrived on that hope. But luck itself wasn't habitual, and he knew that what passed for luck was often something else: cheating. And there was the other kind of luck, the kind he himself possessed, but it depended not on chance but on who and what he was. He knew it was an innate power and not Dame Fortune's erratic smile. Since power like his was rare, the odds made it likely the woman he'd been watching was merely a very clever cheat.

Her skill could provide her with a very good living, he thought, doing some swift calculations in his head. Five grand a week equaled $260,000 a year, and that was just from his casino. She probably hit them all, careful to keep the numbers relatively low so she stayed under the radar.

He wondered how long she'd been taking him, how long she'd been winning a little here, a little there, before Al noticed.

The curtains were open on the wall-to-wall window in his office, giving the impression, when one first opened the door, of stepping out onto a covered balcony. The glazed window faced west, so he could catch the sunsets. The sun was low now, the sky painted in purple and gold. At his home in the mountains, most of the windows faced east, affording him views of the sunrise. Something in him needed both the greeting and the goodbye of the sun. He'd always been drawn to sunlight, maybe because fire was his element to call, to control.

He checked his internal time: four minutes until sundown. Without checking the sunrise tables every day, he knew exactly when the sun would slide behind the mountains. He didn't own an alarm clock. He didn't need one. He was so acutely attuned to the sun's position that he had only to check within himself to know the time. As for waking at a particular time, he was one of those people who could tell himself to wake at a certain time, and he did. That talent had nothing to do with being Raintree, so he didn't have to hide it; a lot of perfectly ordinary people had the same ability.

He had other talents and abilities, however, that did require careful shielding. The long days of summer instilled in him an almost sexual high, when he could feel contained power buzzing just beneath his skin. He had to be doubly careful not to cause candles to leap into flame just by his presence, or to start wildfires with a glance in the dry-as-tinder brush. He loved Reno; he didn't want to burn it down. He just felt so damn *alive* with all the sunshine pouring down that he wanted to let the energy pour through him instead of holding it inside.

This must be how his brother Gideon felt while pulling lightning, all that hot power searing through his muscles, his veins. They had this in common, the connection with raw power. All the members of the far-flung Raintree clan had some power, some heightened ability, but only members of the royal family could channel and control the earth's natural energies.

Dante wasn't just of the royal family, he was the Dranir, the leader of the entire clan. "Dranir" was synonymous with king, but the position he held wasn't ceremonial, it was one of sheer power. He was the oldest son of the previous Dranir, but he would have been passed over for the position if he hadn't also inherited the power to hold it.

Behind him came Al's distinctive knock on the door. The outer office was empty, Dante's secretary having gone home hours before. "Come in," he called, not turning from his view of the sunset.

The door opened, and Al said, "Mr. Raintree, this is Lorna Clay."

Dante turned and looked at the woman, all his senses on alert. The first thing he noticed was the vibrant color of her hair, a rich, dark red that encompassed a multitude of shades from copper to burgundy. The warm amber light danced along the iridescent strands, and he felt a hard tug of sheer lust in his gut. Looking at her hair was almost like looking at fire, and he had the same reaction.

The second thing he noticed was that she was spitting mad.

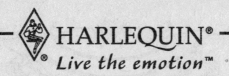

Harlequin® Historical
Historical Romantic Adventure!

Imagine a time of chivalrous knights and unconventional ladies, roguish rakes and impetuous heiresses, rugged cowboys and spirited frontierswomen— these rich and vivid tales will capture your imagination!

Harlequin Historical . . . they're too good to miss!

HHDIR06

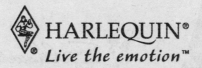